T0063938

FREE AT LAST

LAST

Joni

CLEO FORD

BALBOA.
PRESS

A DIVISION OF HAY HOUSE

Balboa Press books may be ordered through booksellers or by contacting:

Balboa Press
A Division of Hay House
1663 Liberty Drive
Bloomington, IN 47403
www.balboapress.com
1 (877) 407-4847

Because of the dynamic nature of the Internet, any web addresses or
links contained in this book may have changed since publication and
may no longer be valid. The views expressed in this work are solely those
of the author and do not necessarily reflect the views of the publisher,
and the publisher hereby disclaims any responsibility for them.

The author of this book does not dispense medical advice or prescribe the use
of any technique as a form of treatment for physical, emotional, or medical
problems without the advice of a physician, either directly or indirectly. The
intent of the author is only to offer information of a general nature to help
you in your quest for emotional and spiritual well-being. In the event you use
any of the information in this book for yourself, which is your constitutional
right, the author and the publisher assume no responsibility for your actions.

Any people depicted in stock imagery provided by Thinkstock are
models, and such images are being used for illustrative purposes only.
Certain stock imagery © Thinkstock.

Print information available on the last page.

ISBN: 978-1-5043-5136-2 (sc)
ISBN: 978-1-5043-5137-9 (e)

Balboa Press rev. date: 03/11/2016

CHAPTER 1

Mary woke up early and began to cry again for her mother, she remembered last night going to bed and her mother leaving her with her grandmother to go back home to New York without her. Her mother's name was Arabell and everyone called her Bell and her dad was Jacob whom they all called Jake. She could not understand why she could just be left like she was not loved she was only 5 and had never been away from her mother before. Her grandmother lived in Butler, Georgia with her grandfather and two of her cousins whom were both older than she was. She was 5 and very small for her age, she had real dark skin like her dad and often heard family members remarking about how dark she was with such beautiful long black hair. She had come with her mother on the train to have a funeral for her mother's sister who was the mother of her two cousins William and Pearl, William was 7 and Pearl 8, and they both were very upset about seeing their mother in a casket just laying there dead. They had been staying with their grandma Katie and Grandpa Henry every since their mother had gotten sick with pneumonia about a month ago. Mary knew this because she heard the old people talking and saying it would be a good idea for Mary to stay with them for a while because both of them were very fond of their little cousin. Grandma Katie and Grandpa Henry was Mary's mother's parents and Mary had only known a little about them. Mary had been down south to visit a few times when her aunt Bessie her mother's sister was still alive but she always went home with her mother, she was her mother's baby, she was born on November 24, 1942, her family always told her that she was born the day before Thanksgiving. She had an older brother Jacob and an older sister Sadie and she was the third child in the family. Mary did not know anything about death and this was her first experience and just seeing her aunt lying in a casket and that lying in the front room so still just scared her to death. She did not want to fall asleep with that dead body in the next room and her mother laid down with her that night before the funeral and held her until she fell asleep, now her mother was gone and her grandma and grandpa could not comfort her like her mother did. She wanted to go back home to her house where it was not so dark and scary, they had no street lights, nor paved roads and she was just afraid of the dark. All of her aunts and uncles and also her cousins spoke different from her and she had never been away from her mom and it was just awful. Mary's earliest memory when she was about 3 was moving to New York, she did not remember anything of living in the south. Mary did not remembering hearing anything from her mother for a long time a long time, in Mary's mind that could have been a week or a month or a year she just did not remember. She does remember one or two phone calls, but what was said she just does not remember, sometimes she wish she could because she would like to have known if anything was said about coming home.

She does remember starting school and not liking it one bit, first it was on a country road and she does not remember kindergarten, she does remember a class room with children older than her and younger and after awhile she really did get a long with William and Pearl also William was in the same class room with her and would help her with her reading and arithmetic. Mary also got to like feeding the chickens, hogs, and other animals on the farm, she never heard her grandparents speak about her mother and so she did not speak about her, in her childlike mind she thought that her mother did not love her anymore and that is why she left her all alone. Mary began to get use to living in the south and began to learn southern ways as to why when she was in town with her grandma or grandpa she had to move aside to let white people walk by and how she had to drink water out of a fountain that said colored water she really thought the water was like kool aid or something and use to ask her grandparents about such things and they would always reply that is just how it is in the south. Mary's grandparents use to pick cotton and after a while she was required to do the same along with her cousins and would be taken out of school to do so, she hated it, it was hot in those fields and she use to cut her fingers a lot of the time. When Mary did go to school they had a long walk and the school bus with white children on it use to pass them by and they had to jump out of the way because the bus did not slow down for them and the white children use to holler out the windows calling them niggers. Mary did not know what a nigger was and use to ask her cousins and they would tell her colored people were called niggers. Mary's mother and father were both born in Butler, Georgia because her grandmother told her so and use to tell her that her mother was a smart girl but did not get to go to school because she had to help work in the field and also in the white people's house cleaning and helping to take care of their children. Her grandfather had a large family and picking cotton and being submissive to the meager earnings that he was paid for his labor was not what he wanted for his sons and daughters. When Mary's mother and father got married when they were just 15 and 17 one of their goals was to get out of the south. They had heard that life was so much better up north, that there were no fields to work in that there were scrap yards and mills in Pennsylvania and that you made so much more money and lived in real houses with running water and toilets inside. They could not imagine a life like that after being in the south all of their lives. So Mary's father moved his young wife and 3 children to New York looking for a better way to live like so many other southern people were doing. Jake moved to New York in 1918 and brought his family, he had 3 children Jacob Jr, Sadie and Mary. His wife's sister was already living in New York and she had sent for her sister. When Bell moved to New York with her husband he already had family living in New York also, so that is why he also chose New York and also his brother Malcolm told him how great things were up north. He could not wait to find out for himself. It was hard at first with 3 children and a fourth grade education. When Frances, Bell's sister died down south, she took Mary with her to go to the funeral, and that is when she left her there with her grandmother. Mary was too young to know why she was left down south and always felt that she was not loved like her siblings. When Mary was ten she was taken to Atlanta, Georgia to live with another aunt whose name was Thelma and also a sister of her mother's who did not have any children. Mary was given anything she wanted right away hoping that she would not miss her grandparents and cousins as much. Again the crying for her cousins William and Pearl .and her grandparents began she had spent 5 years with them in Butler and even though she was not crazy about Butler she did love her family and after 5 years of living with them she even had finally gotten use to the darkness and even picking cotton with still no mention of her mother. It was like it was taboo to mention her mother and so she never did, and so began life in Atlanta with Aunt Thelma. Atlanta was different from Butler because this was city where she was living and no animals and cotton and so Mary thought she was up north out of the south because they had paved streets and street lights. Mary had her own room and was registered in grade school in the 5th grade where she excelled very well and after 6th grade she went to Junior High and was very bashful and did not have any friends. She was a small girl for her age and so she always felt a little awkward around the other girls who use to tease her for the way she talked with that southern drawl. Mary played by herself a lot and when her aunt Thelma would try to get her to go out and play with the other kids she just did not want to have anything to do with them. Because this aunt did not have any children of her own and always wanted children she just spoiled Mary with all kinds of toys and the best of clothes. She had her own television set and a typewriter which was not heard of for a black girl to have one of her own. Her aunt also got her a sewing machine and taught her how to sew and make pot holders, and small things for herself and the house. They had a yard and an apple and peach tree in the yard and a beautiful garden with roses and tulips and Mary use to just sit in the back and look at how beautiful her home was, but she always felt like it just did not belong to her. She just did not know this aunt and felt like she was just being shipped around from one family member to another and never being told about her mother and father. She was sad a lot and did not communicate well with her aunt. Mary did alright in school but she was still shy and did not make any friends and if anyone tried to befriend her she would just shy away. Her aunt was very nice to her and she spoiled Mary trying to give her all the things that she would have given to her own child but she did not have any children and was glad for the opportunity to spoil her niece. Mary eventually became friendly with one girl she had met at church and she became very close with her and they went to each other's house and played together all the time. Mary excelled well in school and loved going to school, she was very well mannered and dressed very nice, her aunt bought her all kinds of nice things, she had more shoes than she could count, she had play clothes, school clothes and church clothes. She ate very good meals always eggs, grits, bacon, sausage, pancakes, waffles and cold and hot cereal for breakfast. She bought hot lunch at school and always had great dinners, chicken, pork chops, steak, liver and onions, greens, cabbage, okra and tomatoes, rice, and plenty of sweet things like pound cakes, sweet potato pies, lemon meringue pies and plenty of peach and apple cobblers. Mary's friend was named Ruth and she also came from a very nice home with a mom and dad and an older sister whose name was Lydia. Lydia was also very nice to Mary and use to take both of the girls to Sunday school where Mary first learned the story of Jesus. When she went to church in the south they did not go to Sunday school, only church on Sundays, in the morning and in the evening and church on Wednesday s. While she was living with her aunt Mary she went to church four or five times a week and Mary loved it, she had friends at church and they did not pick on her or call her names or even question her about why she did not live with her parents. Mary hated that question more than anything, she felt bad not only because she did not know the answer but also she did not like to think about why she was not loved and wanted by her parents. Mary just started getting into the routine of school, church and play which she did a lot of, when school was not in she did a lot of playing at her friend's house and out on outings with her and her parents. Her aunt worked so when she was at work Mary would stay over her girlfriend's house because her mother was always home, her father was a dentist so they would do a lot of outdoor activities. They went to the amusement park and ate cotton candy, peanuts, popcorn and hot dogs and ice cream, they went to the zoo and seen a lot of different animals like lions, tigers, elephants and monkeys, not chickens, cows and pigs like she was using to seeing down south. Mary also stayed busy doing church activities, singing in the choir, and the youth program and Sunday school, also when the holidays came around like Christmas and Easter they had plays and programs they had to rehearse and get ready for and there was always a big feast after these programs and Ruth's mother always played a big part in these celebrations. They also had big fund raisers to help the poor and needy and Mary really like doing these things, especially going down to the homeless shelter on Thanksgiving and Christmas and feeding the homeless holiday meals. She really liked doing this and started visiting some of the sick and shut in with Ruth and her mother and also doing odd jobs around their houses or going to the store for them and it gave her such a good feeling to think that she was helping someone in need. She had learned in Sunday school that God wanted us to help our brothers and sisters in need and she really felt close to Jesus when she did these things. One of the houses that Ms. Lydia went to regularly she started taking Mary along with her and the old lady's name was Ms. Hattie that lived at the house and she really liked Mary and wanted her to come with Ms. Lydia when Ms. Lydia came to her home. One day Ms. Lydia could not make it and so she asked Mary's Aunt Thelma if it would be alright if she dropped Mary off to spend some time with Ms. Hattie and she would pick her up a little later. Aunt Thelma was pleased with the way Mary got along so well with Ms. Lydia and Ruth that she readily agreed. Mary began visiting Ms. Hattie every Sunday after church taking her a delicious Sunday meal her aunt had cooked; it was usually fried chicken, greens, potato salad, corn bread and pound cake. Ms Hattie would be waiting patiently for Mary to come and Mary would sit down with her while she ate and after Ms. Hattie ate she would always tell Mary stories about how she was raised up in Macon Georgia picking cotton and not being able to go to school because she was needed to pick cotton and she said she also went along with her mother to the white people's homes and helped watched the children while her mother cooked, cleaned and took care of their children. She said when her mother would come home she would be dead tired and then would have to take care of her own family of 7 before falling into bed exhausted to get up at 5 am and start all over again. Ms Hattie was 98 and did not have any children of her own, she had lost her husband after 75 years of marriage 5 years ago and he would have been 100 now if he was still alive. Ms. Hattie talked lovingly of her husband and said that he was such a good man, he was a God fearing man and he loved the Lord and was a deacon at the church that Mary and Ms. Lydia and her daughter Ruth belonged to. Mary also wanted to join that church because she fell in love with the members of that church and also the pastor and his family. She had made plans to talk about it with her aunt but was not sure how to bring up the subject, her aunt went to church but she was not into it like Ms. Lydia and Ruth were. One day at the end of service the pastor began to invite people who were not saved to come to the Lord and give their life to Jesus so that they would be saved and go to Heaven. Now Mary always wanted to go up when she heard this invitation because her and Ruth talked a lot about being saved and not to have to worry about going to hell when she died, whenever that day would come because the pastor always told the congregation that day was coming for each and everyone of us and we never knew when that day would come. Only person Mary knew that had come forward that day was another young girl that was in their Sunday school class, Mary surely did not know if her Aunt was saved or not but did not think so because she did not go to church although she did read her Bible and pray a lot, but she knew she wanted to be saved so this particular Sunday Mary just got up out of her seat and walked down the front of the church and Ms. Lydia and

Ruth were both crying and thanking Jesus for saving Mary's soul. When Mary got home to her aunt's house she was hesitant in telling her aunt because she did not know where her aunt stood on this, but she had promised Ms. Lydia that she would tell her aunt, and so she did and her aunt was very happy for her and told her that she was responsible enough to make a decision about her life and where she wanted to spend eternity at. When school started after summer vacation Mary was in Junior High she had already turned 11, she was also in class with Ruth so it really made it easier to go to a new school, Ruth did not have a lot of friends because she was kind of sheltered, her mom did not allow her to just associate with anyone, her mom knew any girls that she associated with and they were all from the church and they were also her age or very close in age. Ms Lydia also knew their parents and just what kind of background they came from and if it was not a Christian one then she was not allowed to associate with them. That was alright with Ruth because it has always been like that so she was use to it. Mary fell right in line with these rules and regulations and most of the time it was just the two girls that were always together. They use to get teased at school sometimes but most of the time the other children just left them alone and called them Jesus freaks. The school year went pretty fast and it was summer again and the girls were just as tight as ever and Mary continued to visit with Ms. Hattie. One day her aunt Thelma sat her down and told her that her beloved Ms. Hattie had passed away that she just died in her sleep. Well Mary was devastated she had not missed a Sunday in over a year, she was now 12 years old and began to question God about why people died she knew

Ms. Hattie was old but William and Pearl's mother was not old and no one ever said anything about how or why she died. Mary cried so hard and would not eat anything until she made herself sick. She had to take to the bed, she had chills and a fever and her aunt became very concerned and the doctor called which he said it was a bad case of depression along with people that she loved leaving her or dying. Mary did not attend the wake or the funeral she was just too sick to do anything. She could not keep any food down so the doctor put her on liquids and prescribed her some medicine to help with the very sad feeling of losing Ms. Hattie. Ms. Lydia tried to talk with her and tell her that Ms. Hattie would not want her to be sick on account of her and that Ms. Hattie was in Heaven with Jesus and her spirit was with Mary, but Mary had a hard time accepting that. Eventually Mary got better and things got back to normal but Mary did not want to visit any sick and shut in anymore, she did not want to get attached to any old person because it was not a good feeling when they died.

CHAPTER 2

A few more years passed and Mary was now 15 when her Aunt Thelma sat her down one day and told her that her father was coming to pick her up and take her back to New York with him. Mary was devastated she had not heard a word from her parents in ten years and just out of the blue they were here talking about they coming to pick her up. Her mother was not with her father and Mary did not know this man from a hole in the wall and just flat out refused to go into the room and talk with him. Her aunt tried explaining to her that she had no control and was not her legal guardian in anyway and if she could do anything about the situation she would never let Mary go back with him. Mary was so upset she did not even ask about her mother, this man was by himself, he was a complete stranger to her and she just cried and pleaded and it just broke her Aunt Thelma's heart that she had to see her niece go through this and Ms. Lydia and Ruth were both heart broken and could not hide their tears, there were just no words to say how they all felt about Mary leaving and returning to New York, and so they went back to New York where the rest of her immediate family lived. Mary cried all the way New York and nothing this strange man sitting beside her could say that would make her feel better, she had really loved her aunt and did not know her mom and dad, her aunt cried also because she loved the child and did not want her to leave. Mary did not know why she had to leave and was afraid to ask, she did get a chance to say goodbye to her friends Ms. Lydia and Ruth and they both just hugged her and cried. Mary did not say a word to this stranger all the way home even though he kept trying to talk with her. He told her that her mother had passed, she still did not say a word, Mary felt she did not know this man and was very upset in the way they just gave her away and now showing up making her come back with him, never a thought of how she felt, well here is how she felt she thought to herself she was five when they brought her here left her with her aunt and she had no say so and she was 15 now and had plenty of say so. Mary had decided that she was going to run away she had no intention of staying with this stranger and she had no feelings about a mother she never heard about and did not even remember what she looked like, what kind of mother could do that to her 5 year old baby. Her father kept trying to make conversation telling her that there were certain things that she would never understand about her mother and why they did not keep in contact with her over the years. Mary did not want to hear it and she had cried all she was going to cry over her immediate family and had no tears left just a hate feeling that she had never felt in her lifetime and it did not feel good, but she just did not know what to do with these feelings. It took them about 8 or 9 hours to get to New York where her family lived on 22nd Street in Brooklyn, New York and Mary never seen anything so dirty in her life, the streets were just filthy and people looked just as filthy also. These people were so poor and the streets were so dirty and so many people, people everywhere, she thought Atlanta had a lot of people but in Atlanta she lived in a very nice neighborhood with beautiful homes and tree lined streets and all of the people had beautiful homes and garages for their cars. These houses in Brooklyn were connected together and she did not see any back yards or patios with sliding glass doors, this was just the pits and she had her nose turned up from the time her father pulled in front of one of those houses and said you are home, she still had not said one word and did not want to get out of the car, but her father opened the door and pulled her out. It seemed like a bunch of people came out the front door and just stared at her and she just glared right back at them, she heard one girl looked to be about her age say what's her problem, her father just said shut up Emily and get back in the house. Mary was short and this girl was tall and looked about 12 or 13, she just turned up her nose and went into the house followed by a group of people. After getting her things out of the car and carrying them into the house her father just said everyone this is Mary your sister that has been living down in Atlanta with your Aunt Thelma. Mary felt so awkward standing in front of these strangers and they all looking at her like she was some kind of freak, then an older lady came up to her and said hi Mary I am your grandmother Irene and your dad Jacob is my son, my only child please feel welcome we are glad to have you here. Mary just looked at her and did not blink an eye or say a word, her grandmother said honey it will take a little time but you will get use to us, we are family this is your dad's side of the family, I have brothers and sisters and they all have kids we are planning a big celebration for you so that you can meet everyone and she asked Mary to please try and relax that everything was going to be alright, her son had told her that Mary had not said one word the whole trip and had not eaten anything. She tried to get Mary to please eat something and maybe she would feel a little better about meeting her family who were looking forward to her coming to New York. Mary never said a word, when she was living in Atlanta she really felt at home, not in this place she had left her family in Atlanta and that was where she wanted to go back to she did not know these people and did not want to get to know them either. When she was only 5 and did not remember her siblings at all, and now they were trying to introduce her to this brand new world and wanted her to fit right in like it was only a couple of years that she has been gone, not the ten that she actually had been gone and had not heard a word from these people, no way was she going to accept this. No one talked about her brother or sister that she could hardly remember or her mother for that fact, her dad just started introducing her to these people some lady name Sara (her stepmother) Emily 10, Beverly 9, Charles 11, and Jake Jr., 15 her age and these other children belonged to her it was just too much to take in all at one time, and her brother Jake and sister Sadie they were just not around anymore and how could there be two Jake Juniors belonging to her dad she did not bother to ask because she still was not talking to these people. That really frightened Mary's family because they had not been around her and had not seen this type of behavior before and decided to let her alone for awhile and thought that she would eventually warm up to them. Mary sat on a chair in their front room and just stared ahead,

Grandma fixed something to eat and ask Mary did she want to eat, Mary did not answer she just stared ahead, after about four hours of her not moving had not even ask to go to the bathroom her grandma decided to call her Aunt Thelma in Atlanta and see if she could talk with her but Mary refused to even get up and take the phone. The family did not know what to do they thought they would just have to wait it out, but Mary was being very stubborn she finally had to go to the bathroom but instead of asking anyone where it was she just got up and began looking around the house until she found the bathroom. Mary was thinking to hell with them she did not want to be there and had no intention on staying, she did not know what her next move would be but she was going to stay and think it through before she just started wandering the streets of New York. She could tell by the ride through the neighborhood with her dad that she was actually afraid to death of this big city with all of these strange people even the ones in her family. Mary finally fell to sleep sitting on the sofa and when her grandmother tried to wake her up to go to bed she just refused and stayed right there on the sofa all night. She slept really hard because when she woke up it was to smell of bacon frying and she could hear the rustling around in the kitchen and a little bit of the conversation about whether or not she would be hungry enough to eat something. Mary was very hungry but she was also very stubborn, she had not eaten in almost two days and she was starving but she just refused to move off the sofa and let them see her weakness for something to eat. Mary had money so she just got up off the sofa and walked out the door while they were in the kitchen cooking, she was amazed to see the same dirty streets and people sitting out so early in the morning on their stoops and staring at her. She just started to walk down the street and made a right turn on to the main street, she made sure she looked at the numbers and street names so that she could find her way back. There were stores everywhere so she went into one and bought a soda and some junk food, as she was coming out of the store she seen her father coming down the street and he was very angry telling her that she could not just go walking around New York this was not Atlanta and anything could happen to her he asked her did she understand, she never said a word, he still did not know what her voice sound like. After Mary got back she ate her junk food and drank her soda and just sat there, her father told her you are going to have to take a shower and told her where the towels and wash clothes were, she still just stared right through him, he just hunched his shoulder and went into the kitchen with the other family members where they were still eating. Mary just sat there eventually the rest of the family members came into the front room and started watching television or just looking at her. Her dad left and was gone most of the morning until early afternoon and in between that time her grandmother attempted to talk with her again saying child tell grandma what is wrong we know you can talk because you were talking just fine before you left Atlanta, Mary still just sat there staring into space. Mary was upset with her aunt for letting this happen and more than a little upset with her dad's family who just took her down south and left her there and not a word in ten years what kind of people does this kind of thing and expect everything to be just alright, well they would see that it was not alright if they expected her to welcome them with open arms she would show them. It was the beginning of summer and school was out for the summer so she did not know if this was suppose to be over the summer to see if everything worked out for a summer visit or a permanent situation it did not matter she wanted no parts of this arrangement. By suppertime Mary had not moved and her grandmother just told her that if she got hungry to go into the kitchen and fix her plate because she did not want to fix one for her not knowing what she liked and disliked and how much she could eat. Mary never said a word just kept watching television and watching the other kids as they came and went all day even her father came in and left quite a few times and did not say anymore to her since he had hollered at her that morning for leaving the house without telling anyone. Mary don't know what time she fell asleep but when she woke up she was the only one downstairs and so she went into the kitchen and made a plate of food. There was a small pot with spaghetti in it a salad in the refrigerator, she put the spaghetti in the microwave and warmed it up and put some dressing on the salad and ate it, and Mary was really hungry she also found something to drink. After eating her food she went back to the couch and watched T.V. until she fell to sleep and she slept so soundly she did not hear her grandmother come downstairs and go into the kitchen and fix breakfast and gradually the rest of the family members began to come down and they all sat at the table and ate, her grandmother asked her to join them but she did not say a word just sat there. After breakfast her grandmother told her she would go upstairs and take a shower or she would drag her upstairs and give her one, she gave her a choice. After every one had left out of the kitchen Mary went in and fixed herself a bowl of cereal and then made her way upstairs to the bathroom and took a shower and looked into her luggage to get clean clothes and threw her dirty things into the hamper and came back downstairs and resumed her spot on the sofa not saying a word to anyone. The youngest of her siblings came and sat by Mary and told her name was Beverly and she wanted to be friends with her and take her out to meet her friends, but Mary just looked at her and never said a word. Beverly asked her "can you talk or are you deaf and dumb" Mary just stared at her just then Emily walked in and said "daddy said to leave her alone: so Beverly got up and went outside to play. Mary continued this silent routine and got into a real routine of staying on the couch, getting up to fix her food when everyone was out of the kitchen, taking showers, sleeping on the sofa and only going out to get personal needs, deodorant, shampoo, lotion, pads for when she had her monthly but still never said a word, when she would go into the store she would just pick up what she needed pay for it and leave. Days turned into weeks and weeks into months and before you knew it time for school came around. When her father approached her about school Mary was still not talking, her father told her that she would be made to go to school because that was what she had to do because it was the law, she still never said a word, it had been 3 months and she had not said one word. Mary was afraid to get attached to anyone because she never knew if or when she would be snatched up and moved somewhere else again, she never told her dad this but she felt it. By this time Mary was going to be 16 in a couple of months and suppose to be going to high school and she was not looking forward to it, she did not know what she was going to do when her dad made her go to school but she was plotting something, what she did know was that she did not want to go to school. Her father enrolled her in school and the school district got her records from her Jr. High School in Atlanta and shared with her father that Mary was a straight A student and they would be so pleased to have her attend their High school which was a brand new school in Brooklyn, because most of the schools in Brooklyn were old and run down. This was 1957 and Mary had always been sheltered Mary was just a scared little girl, she never looked her age people always thought she was 10 or 11 because that was the way she looked she had just started having her menstrual period when she was almost 15. She had just recently started to develop and wear a training bra that her Aunt Thelma had bought for her whereas her friend Ruth was having her menstrual at age 11 so Mary always thought she was a little different from girls her age. The first day of school her father took her to school but the other children were allowed to walk, Jacob was the only one who went to her school, her dad went to her class with her and explained to the teacher that Mary was real shy and was not talking to anyone not even his family since leaving Atlanta at the beginning of summer, he said she was upset and for the school to give her a little time to adjust and he was sure she would start to talk. When her dad left her at the school he told her that he would be back to get her at the end of the day and where to wait for him at, he also said that Jacob would keep a eye on her and wait with her until he got there to pick her up, he hugged her and told her that he loved her, she was very stiff and did not say a word. Mary went to her class and sat down, the teacher Miss Jenkins introduced herself to the class and welcomed them all, she told them that Mary Robinson was new to New York and that she moved here from Atlanta and that some of them probably knew her brother Jake Robinson she asked one of the girls name Cynthia Smith to kind of show her around until she became familiar with the school. Now Cynthia was a nice girl and between classes she tried to strike up a conversation with Mary but Mary still was not talking to anyone so Cynthia just gave her some space as Miss Jenkins had suggested she felt like Mary just needed sometime. Well the first day went pretty good, her brother found out what her last class was and was at her locker to meet her, he tried asking her how was her first day but she still was not talking. Their father came to pick them up and so went the first day of school, but everything was still the same at the house, she ate after everyone else had eaten and they all had chores except her and she never slept upstairs she really liked sleeping downstairs by herself, eventually they began to open the couch into a bed and that became her bed at night. The next day at school went similar to the first, in the cafeteria Cynthia sat with Mary and tried to make conversation with her, Miss Jenkins had told her what Mary's father had told her about how Mary had not spoken to anyone all summer long because she was upset that she had to leave Atlanta to come and live in New York. Mary did her school work without talking with anyone and by now the whole class knew that she could talk but just refused to talk with anyone. Mary went to school where all of the students were black, there they taught the students sewing and cooking, along with typing and shorthand which Mary loved and did very well in. Her father did not want her just learning how to cook and sew, he also made sure that she had a language because he knew how important it was for her to have a language to get into a good college. Her dad explained to the school that he wanted his daughter to learn a skill that would help her after high school. Mary became a very good typist and loved typing and she use to daydream about working in an office and typing. Mary was sheltered in her life and did not understand that black girls did not get jobs typing in offices in the 60's. Her father was very strict on his girls and they were only allowed to stay close in the neighborhood, they were not allowed to roam all over the city, he knew first hand how dangerous it was out in the streets and he wanted to protect his girls from that danger. He was often heard saying that oldest daughter got away but the rest of them would not. After about a couple of months into school life right before her 16th birthday Mary began to talk, the first words out of her mouth was to her friend Cynthia in school one day, Cynthia was talking about her Sunday school lesson and Mary just said "I use to love Sunday school when I lived in Atlanta and that is one of the things that I miss the most is my church" well that started a big conversation between the girls, Mary told Cynthia that she use to sing in the choir and also joined a singing group that use to go around to different events singing spiritual songs. Cynthia was glad to know that Mary was saved and loved church like she did, she was also glad that she was the one that Mary opened up to and the first to hear her speak. After that the two girls began to talk and talk all through the lunch period when they got back to their homeroom class Cynthia could not wait to tell Ms. Jenkins that Mary had talked and had opened up to her and Ms. Jenkins was so happy and asked Mary would she also talk with her, Mary liked Ms. Jenkins and opened up to her also about why she refused to talk for such a long period, she thought that her dad would take her back to Atlanta if she seemed sad and would not talk to anyone. When Mary's dad came to pick her up she said "hi dad" and her father did a double take and just looked at Mary and said "you can talk O my God, I really thought you had lost your voice girl" "well thank God" he said, he told her the rest of the family will sure be glad that you have finally opened your mouth and can actually talk. He wanted to know what all the silence was about and Mary told him that she just did not want to come to New York and she was more upset about no one even contacting her in the last ten years and she asked her dad what was that all about. He promised her that he would tell her all about it but this was not the time and he only wanted it to be her and him when he talked to her, because Jake Jr. was with them. When they got home he hollered for his mom to come into the living room and told his daughter to speak to his mom and Mary said "hi grandma and I am sorry for not talking with you all this time". Her grandma ran and hugged her granddaughter and just cried and said "thank you Jesus, I thought something was wrong with my child. As the different family members came in she spoke with each one of them and apologized to each and everyone and everyone, except her stepmother was overjoyed. Her stepmom said "well it's about damn time", and her dad spoke right up and said "don't you dare say one negative thing to my child, you ran off one but I will be damned if you do anything to hurt this one, you can just forget it". Mary looked in shock and her dad said "don't worry baby everything is going to be fine, if anyone leaves it will be her". Everyone got really quite and her grandmother broke the spell by telling everyone dinner would be ready in a short while and they would all be looking forward to having Mary at the dinner table. At dinner that night Beverly made sure to sit next to her sister Mary she was so happy to have Mary at the table and Mary was talking to everyone and apologizing over and over for acting the way she did being a Christian and all that was not the way she was raised. Everyone was just glad to hear her talking and she let everyone know that she loved dinner which was baby lima beans cooked with ham hocks, rice and corn bread that was the kind of meal she was use to and hot right off of the stove not warmed up in the oven. After dinner her grandma showed her which room she would be sleeping in, she was going to be sharing a room with Beverly and Emily, Beverly was just insisting that they share a room and Emily wanted her own room even though she had warmed up to her sister also along with the rest of the family except her mother was still real cold toward Mary. Mary could care less because she was just a stepmom anyway and if she did not like her that was her problem, Mary was just glad that everyone was so forgiving. Mary and Beverly talked late into the night all about Atlanta and Beverly told her about New York, they talked until they fell asleep and they were going to have to get up early for school the next day. The next morning Mary was allowed to walk to school with Jake and some of his friends, her father trusted her to walk with her brother and his friends and he promised her that she would be expected to call her Aunt Thelma and talk with her, Mary was excited about that and could not wait. At school a lot of the children crowded around Mary and began to talk at once, Ms. Jenkins ask them to give her some space and that Mary was glad to talk with everyone that wanted to talk but it would have to wait until recess, changing of classes and lunch time. No one was more thrilled than Cynthia because she is the one that Mary opened up to first so she really felt privileged for all the attention Mary was getting it was like she had gotten her to talk when no one else could. Mary called her aunt Thelma the next day and they just cried on the phone her aunt was so glad to hear from her and told her Ms. Lydia and Ruth asked about her all the time. She asked Mary had her father talked to her about her mom and sister and brother but he had not done so yet she told her but that he said he would soon he just needed the right time. She told her aunt that everything at school was going well and that she had a new friend that was a Christian and she was hoping to go to church with her soon because her dad and his side of the family did not attend church. Her aunt did not seem to surprised about it because she knew a lot about this family and knew they were not church going people and she told Mary not to stop praying and try to get back into church and that she hoped that she could see her niece soon, Mary told her she would like that a lot and she really did miss them and that is why she had stopped talking because she was so upset that she was made to leave them in such a hurry and no explanation but she said she was all over that and ready to move on in life.

CHAPTER 3

Mary did start going to church with Cynthia in North Brooklyn to Cynthia's family's church called Pinkett Tabernacle Church it was a very small family like church and Mary got to know all the other families also she met Cynthia's mother Mrs. Brown and her brothers, James and Robert and Charles was close to her age and very nice looking and Mary was still shy when it came to boys because she had never really even talked to boys before. She liked Cynthia's mother right away, Ms. Brown was a very friendly lady and made Mary welcome in their home, they lived in a small apartment and Mary wondered where everyone slept, they did not have a upstairs and downstairs like her house instead they lived on the second floor and more than once she wanted to ask Cynthia where everyone slept but was to embarrassed. After Mary started to go to church her father did not object even though his family did not attend any church, this was a few months after Mary started talking and she also began to go to Sunday school every Sunday. Mary did not live very far from Cynthia but her father had gotten in the habit of dropping her off and picking her up. Mary's new friend Cynthia lived on Montgomery Avenue at 22nd Street and Mary lived at 18th Street. Cynthia's mother loved the Lord; one of those old time religion kind of families. On any Sunday morning one could hear her mother's gospel music coming from their windows, especially in the summer, when their windows were wide open. Cynthia became her first real friend. She was tall and slim even at 14 years old, with skin that was a pretty creamy milk chocolate Cynthia did not go to parties and dances like the other girls at school because she was saved and was not interested in those types of worldly things and the kids at school thought that Cynthia was a little stuck up so they began to associate that same feeling toward Mary and so Mary did not have a lot of friends at school which was just fine with her. She had met some of her cousins on her dad's side of the family, he had 1 brother whose name was Johnny and 2 sisters Evelyn and Nora, her uncle Johnny had 10 children her aunts did not have any. These were Jacob's half brother and sisters not his mother Irene's children but she called them her children and when her and her husband came north the girls came with them and Johnny came later with 3 children, the rest were born in New York. All three of Jacob's siblings had different mothers and no one ever found out about Evelyn and Nora's mothers but the family knew about Johnny's mother. That is just how it was then in the south and no one in the family questioned anything, it was just one big happy family, although Johnny kept his distance from Grandma Irene him and his brother Jacob got along well. Evelyn and Nora never had children but they were raised by Grandma Irene and always called her mother and never mentioned any other mother. Mary had a cousin that was the same age as Cynthia and herself whose name was Gloria whom everyone called Glo and she was the one that Mary became very close with, they had the same last name Robinson and Gloria was very popular and she was allowed to talk to boys and they did not go to church just like her immediate family did not go to church. The girls would get together and go to the movies or just hang around the neighborhood with a few of Gloria's friends, but mostly Mary just hung out with Cynthia because she felt they had so much in common and they did a lot of church functions singing in the choir, picnics, fun raisers and going around to other churches to fellowship. Mary's family was very supportive of her church activities, her dad just wanted to keep her grounded, so one day he decided it was time to talk about her mother, brother and sister, his mother had been getting on him about putting it off and Mary did not want to bring it up because she was not sure if she wanted to hear what he had to say. He took Mary to a nice restaurant in South Brooklyn that was popular for very good food, New York was known for its delicious food, especially cheese steak hoagies and corn beef hoagies, Mary had not experienced anything like it in Atlanta and they also had very good food there. But her dad took her to a nice sit down restaurant in a nice neighborhood and told her to order anything she wanted off of the menu. This was the first time it was just her and her dad in an atmosphere like this one, the restaurant was elegant and they were dressed up real nice because he had told her this was going to be a special occasion her 17th birthday was coming up in a few days and her dad said he wanted to do something special for her. He seemed like he was always going out of his way to be especially nice to her and her stepmother could not stand her and she did little to hide it, she tried to act like she liked her but everyone in the household knew different, so when he announced that just those two were going out to dinner stepmom just flipped accusing Mary's dad of treating her better than he did the other children. He told her he did not have to defend what he did with his daughter to her and if she did not like it she could get out of his mother's house and he slammed the door as he and Mary left the house. Mary felt bad she did not want to be the reason for any arguments between her dad and stepmom and she told her dad that and he told her not to worry he was sick of that woman anyway and have been for a long time, matter of fact it was the lead he needed to begin to tell her about her own mom and sister and brother but first he wanted them to order dinner and eat and then they could talk. Mary ordered Delmonico steak, fries, salad and broccoli and her dad ordered lamb chops, mashed potatoes, salad and broccoli and as they waited for their meal the waitress brought them hot rolls and drinks, they both had soda and they made small talk about church, school, boys and friends that Mary had made since being with her dad for 2 years. It did not seem that long but Mary had really started to like New York, it was rough but it also was a special place with a lot of opportunities if you were looking for them. They had a good teaching hospital and great colleges and their public schools were also highly rated for being schools in the city. After dinner and over dessert which was hot apple pie and vanilla ice cream, Mary's dad cleared his throat and begin talking he started by telling Mary that this was a very touchy subject and one he wish he did not have to have with his daughter but knew that it was necessary in order for him to feel satisfied with himself and to give his daughter answers to questions that have been too long coming. He started by saying your mother loved you very much and when she took you to Georgia she wanted you to be with her family because she was very sick and she knew that she was dying and did not want you at 5 years old to remember your mother's death. He told her that her mother had breast cancer and the doctors had only given her 6 months to live and that she was also heart broken because he was having an affair with Sara that she had Jacob a few months before I was born and that her stepmom was pregnant with Emily when she took me down south and that Jacob and Sadie were staying at the house with Grandma Irene and him. The stepmom Sara was still down in Butler, Georgia her hometown and that he knew her before he knew my mom because they lived in different parts of Georgia, but Macon was not that far from Butler. He told her that his mom and dad and his two sisters came to New York because his father heard that they were hiring black men to work in the shipyard but he was the baby and was left in Georgia with his grandma Katie, who was Grandma Irene's mom. Jacob and Sadie were 12 and 10 at the time and he had been having an affair with Sara every since he married Mary's mom because she was pregnant with Jacob. He said he loved my mom but he loved Sara also and did not want to give her up and she did not want to give him up even though he was married to my mom. This was a lot for Mary to digest but she was shocked and still wanted to hear more. They finished their dessert and her dad continued to talk telling her that Jacob enlisted into the army when he was 18 and that he was sent to Viet Nam where he was killed and Sadie was just devastated losing her mom, her brother and her baby sister all at once, he said that

Sadie just left home and no one knew or heard anything from her from the time she left home. He continued to tell her that her stepmom came to New York after her mom died and she did not like Sadie, he had been going back and forth to Georgia for years and that her mom Belle knew about the other children he had fathered and she never got over it and that he carried that guilt around for a long time just like he carried the guilt for not coming to get her sooner. He said her stepmom did not want Mary to come home she was always jealous of his kids by her mom and people in the family were whispering that her stepmom had something to do with Sadie's disappearance . Jacob said that he let his wife talk him into leaving Mary with her aunt, he know it was wrong but did not want Sara to mistreat Mary as she had done Sadie. Her dad was asking for her forgiveness and was hoping that they could have a very nice father and daughter relationship and that she could also have a good relationship with her other siblings. Mary told her dad that all of this was a lot to take in at one time but she knew she could not hold this against him because she had learned that holding a grudge against anyone was not a good feeling and it did nothing for you on the inside, she also told her dad that she would just pray for understanding and not try to judge anyone, not even her stepmom and that she knew that it was not going to be easy. He told her to let him handle the stepmom something he should have done a long time ago but that he was just so torn between the two women and after Belle died he just tried to do the right thing with her stepmom by marrying her and giving all her children his last name. He told her another sore spot with him about her stepmom was that he asked her not to name her son Jacob also because he had a son name Jacob and he was the real Junior in the family, but Sara was a real hot head and felt she should have been the only wife and she named her son Jacob Jr. anyway. They had talked so long that the restaurant was getting ready to close and they had no idea so much time had passed, but Mary was so glad for this talk with her father and she had been having more feelings for him the longer she stayed and talked with him that this talk just seemed to push the relationship even closer still. When they got home it was after 11 pm and the house was dark, Mary went up to her room and her dad went to his room. Mary did not see Emily and Beverly in their beds and she went to ask her father where they were, he told her that he did not know for her to go to bed and they would talk in the morning. The next morning was a Sunday so everyone should have been home but only Grandma Irene and her dad were in the kitchen, drinking coffee and talking about where Emily, Beverly, Jacob and their mother were because none of them were at the house. Grandma Irene told them that Sara called her brother down south and had him send enough money for them to go Georgia; she said she had some money but not enough for all of them to catch the train. Mary heard her father say good riddance it should have happened a long time ago and he was not sorry he was just fed up with that woman he said and that he did not love her anymore. He did say that he loved his kids and would miss them very much but this was something that was way overdue, Jacob blamed himself for his wife's suffering and also for not knowing where Sadie is at, if his child is alive and well or dead somewhere it has been 10 years since she has been gone and Jake has had many sleepless nights. His mother comforted her child and told him that we all make mistakes and not to take it so hard if God was willing he would see his child again and that has always been her prayer, as well as her prayer to see Mary again. She loved Sara's children but she always felt that Belle's kids got the short end of the stick and was overjoyed to see her son step up and take control of this situation that he had created. The rest of the day Mary just hung around the house reading and straighten up her room and really enjoying having it all to herself for a while, she did not know how long but she was not concerned about her sisters now that she had her dad all to herself. She did think about her missing sister and prayed that she would see her one day and that she would be fine and glad to see her as well. The next morning the 3 of them Mary, her grandma and her dad had breakfast together and they talked about dinner the night before that the two had and Jake told his mother that he had told his daughter everything, he said he felt like a weight had been lifted off of him. Grandma Irene was happy and said that it had been long enough. Then the conversation got around to Sara and the kids and Grandma also said that the situation between her son and those two wives of his has always been a sore spot in her life, because she did not want to pick sides but that my mother had really gotten the short end of the deal. This conversation later became known as the talk, Jacob even said that he did not love Sara any longer and had been fallen out of love with her and was very glad that all of this came to a head and that she was gone. He did not want to see his children go but if that was the only way he could get rid of their mother then good riddance. After breakfast Mary went up to her room and it felt very good to have so much privacy, she really did miss Beverly because she knew that Beverly was becoming attached to her and really did care about her but she also loved this feeling of freedom. She called Cynthia and they talked for hours on the phone she told her all about the dinner and everything her dad told her she felt very comfortable telling Cynthia her family's private business, she knew she could trust her to keep it to herself. After talking with Cynthia she called her Aunt Thelma and told her everything her dad told her and Aunt Thelma told her that she knew about the history all along but felt it was not her place for her to tell Mary about her dad's side of the family. She told Mary that she is glad that her dad finally told her the reason her mother brought her to them when she knew that she was going to die, she did not want her baby around Sara or her mother-in-law and was sorry that she let the older two stay with their dad and stepmom. After talking with her aunt and best friend Mary got on her knees and prayed and asked God not to let her have any hard feelings toward her stepmom for wrecking her mom's marriage. She asked God to give her love in her heart for Sara even though she knew Sara did not care for her, she knew there was nothing that she could do about the way Sara felt but she did not want to carry around any hard feelings.

CHAPTER 4

For the next year Mary and her father had a wonderful relationship together, they went to basketball games, Mary loved all kinds of sports especially basketball and football, they went to the movies, out to dinner, fishing, all the activities that she was involved in at school and Mary continued to be a straight A student and different colleges began to reach out to her about scholarships and Mary began to get excited about going away to college. In the meantime she was busy with church and she had gotten a part time job at a drugstore and this kept her pretty busy and she was still shy when it came to boys because this was the 60's and it was still not so popular to be as dark as Mary was and for boys to be interested in her. Just about all the girls in 12th grade were going steady, even Cynthia had a boyfriend, even though he was a member of their church and he was considered a nice boy she still had one. Mary acted like it was not a big deal when she talked with Cynthia about not having a boyfriend but secretly she would have liked to have someone interested in her also, at night sometimes she use to think about Charles a lot, he was Cynthia's baby brother but he did not look her way he talked to a lot of the girls at church but treated her like his sister.

Mary became very close with her dad and confided in him a lot about how she felt that none of the boys ever asked her out on a date and here she was almost 18 and had never been kissed, her dad would assure her that time would come for boys and it was no big deal not to have a boyfriend at 17. It did not bother Mary so much that she did not have a boyfriend as much as it bothered her that she would never have a boyfriend because she was so dark and she heard her Grandma Irene always talking about how black she was and some of the kids at school use to snicker behind her back and call her black Mary. When she talked to her dad about it he told her to keep her head up high most of them was jealous because she was a straight A student, a nice girl, dressed nice and had beautiful long black hair and the majority of those girls would die for her hair and Cynthia use to tell her the same thing. But Cynthia did not have a lot of time for her outside of church because she was also working as a nurse's helper after school and on the weekends, plus she had a steady boyfriend from church although she was limited with the amount of time she could spend with him because her parents were also very strict with her being the only girl. Mary continued to busy herself with her job, school and reading and writing poems, something she had just picked up lately but really did like it. Also her father made sure he did some kind of activity with her at lease twice a week so he could keep up on what was going on in her life. Her Grandma Irene kept herself busy writing numbers and selling beer and pop in the neighborhood, it was her way of keeping some change besides a couple days of week she went into the white neighborhood and did days work, that is what it was called, cleaning white women's houses and taking care of their children for a few dollars. Mary was determined that she would never do any such thing her father had put into her that get a good education and you could be all that you could be no matter what color your skin was. Mary's father always told her about being in the army in WWII and how they treated the black solders and just about all of the white solders referred to the black solders as niggers. Jake said that is where he started drinking because he was so miserable and his job was a cook most of the black solders had jobs like that. He said that he tried to go AWOL but got drunk and passed out in one of the bars and woke up in the military hospital, Jake said that was the best day of his life when the war was over in 1945 and he came home to his family, at that time Belle was his one and only love, Sara had Jacob down south while she was still living with her family. He said my stepmom did not come to New York until the following year in 1946 and he began a relationship with her setting her up in an apartment and going between the two families. Sara had her next 3 children in the following 3 years, she had Emily in 1947, Beverly in 1948 and Charles in 1949 she had left Jacob down south with her mother and he was born in 1942 7 months before Mary was born. Mary thought that was just disgusting and did not want to think about how that made her mom feel her knowing all about Sara and about how her dad told her that Sara said she was not going anywhere because Jake belonged to her first even though Belle had 2 children and was married to Jacob and was not married to her when any of her children were born because he had a wife. After a few years Sara got fed up and took her kids and moved back down south because Jacob would not leave his wife and she got tired of sneaking around with him.

Mary thought all that stuff about her having him first did not amount to a hill of beans because she did not get him to marry her so she was the fool to stay in the background and sneak around with Jacob on the side like a fool. Mary could hardly remember her mother but she still could feel empathy for anyone who had a husband that ran around on her and even had a whole family while still having a relationship with both. Mary had promised herself that she would not get caught in those feelings because they did not make her feel good and she did have feelings for her half brother and sisters. Mary was glad of one thing she had her dad all to herself she did not hear anything about Sara and her children, she did think maybe it is time for her and her children to be out of the picture just like she was out of the picture for 10 years. Sara and her children did not come back to New York until Belle died and that is when she moved in with her Grandma Irene to help out as she said, but all she helped do that Mary saw was run her sister off. But she could not dwell on it too much because it would just build up a lot of anger and she really needed someone besides her father to talk to about it. Mary missed her close friendship with Cynthia since they were not together as much as they use to be, she did realize that they were growing up and had separate lives that did not give them time to be with each other like they use to, she did always see Cynthia at Sunday school and church and they would promise to catch up even then Cynthia would sit with her boyfriend at church because he was active at church also.

Summer 1959 ended and it was back to school, Mary could not believe that she was in the 12th grade and this was her last year, She was determined to continue to get straight A's for her last year so that she could get into a good college on a scholarship. All of her teachers told her that she would have no problem getting an academic scholarship to almost the school of her choice and she had a few in mind. She had wanted to go to a black college but she did not want to leave her dad, Mary would not admit it but she was afraid to go away to school and leave her dad, it was a feeling that she could not explain it just hurt deep down even to think of leaving him for 4 years, and of course her dad did not know anything about this they did discuss different colleges that had be recruiting Mary and there were a lot. Jacob just wanted Mary to visit all of the schools that were interested and find out all that each had to offer before she made a selection. Mary did talk to Cynthia about her decision and she had always hoped that they would go to college together and be room mates but Cynthia was not going to college and she did not have much advice for Mary. Cynthia's family could not afford college and Cynthia was really not interested in college Cynthia was more interested in getting married after high school that is all she talked about whenever the girls would talk. Cynthia told Mary that she had started seeing another guy that she really was falling hard for and he was not a church boy like the other boy she had been dating and that her parents were not fond of him at all because he did not go to church. His name she told Mary was James and he worked for city cleaning the streets and he had his own apartment, now she was not allowed to go to his apartment but she would sneak and go and she told Mary that she had sex with him but that they were careful. Mary tried to talk to her friend and told her that was not a good choice she was making and that she should really think twice about her decision to be sexually active. Cynthia told Mary that she was in love with James and he was in love with her and that she would never leave him for her mother or father's sake she said she would be turning 18 soon and that there was nothing they could do about it, she said James had told her the same thing and that he wanted to get married as soon as she graduated from high school. Mary was very upset that Cynthia seems to be changing her way of life because of James, he did not attend church and he went to bars and night clubs and hung and that was not the way Cynthia was raised. Mary tried talking to her dad about her friend and the road that she seen her going down but he told Mary she is going to have to find that out for herself because all she could see right now was this was her first love and she was not interested in anything anyone had to say about it. Cynthia started skipping school and going to James's apartment and having her parents think that she was going to school, eventually they found out because the school called her parents after she started missing so much school. Mary became more involved in school and her job and doing things with her dad that she soon was not talking about Cynthia at all. A few months later she heard that Cynthia was pregnant and was planning on getting married, when she heard that she called Cynthia to see if it was true and Cynthia told her it was and that her parents were very disappointed in her. Cynthia told Mary that the baby was due in June when she was suppose to be graduating but that she would have to go to summer school or night school to get enough credits to get her diploma. Cynthia also said that she would be going to the Justice of the Peace to get married; that she and James were getting their blood tests the following week and the only people that were going to be present was James's parents and her parents. Mary felt so bad for her friend but she knew she had to get on with her life and marriage and babies were a long way off for her, there were a few girls in her class that had gotten pregnant also and dropped out of school.

In June of 1960 Mary graduated with honors and was recruited by Dunbar in New York with a major in Business Management. Mary had visited quite a few colleges but she had made her mind up early that she did not want to leave New York, she was truly a daddy's girl by now and did not want to cut the cord just yet. Mary was always interested in Business Management and had been offered a scholarship to Dunbar School of Business in Washington D.C... Mary was leaning toward this school because it was a very good school and it was in Washington, D.C., she had talked with her father at great lengths about her interest in this school and they went to visit the school and both were impressed with what they saw. Her father, grandmother and her Aunt Thelma were present for her graduation, she was so glad to see her aunt they both just cried and cried tears of joy to see this day come and she told her aunt that she played a big part in her getting the education that she had gotten so far and was determined to make her family very proud of her when she went away to college. Two weeks before graduation on June 6, 1960 Cynthia gave birth to a baby boy whom she named James Owen Green, he weighed 8lbs and 6oz and Cynthia and James were the proud parents. Cynthia asked Mary if she would be the baby's Godmother and Mary jumped at the offer and said she would be honored. Mary went to see her godson and bought the baby a beautiful blue outfit to come home in and a bassinet. Cynthia was happy about having her son, but Mary could see the sadness in her eyes when Mary talked about graduating in two weeks and going to Wharton School of Business Washington, DC in the fall. Mary's father surprised her with a brand new Chevy for a graduation present, she could hardly believe her eyes it was a beautiful red 2 door Chevy Impala with red upholster with a cassette player installed in it. Mary was in Heaven she just hugged and kissed her dad and told him he was the best dad in the world, he had taught her how to drive a year ago and she had just gotten her license earlier in the spring. Her dad told her that she had to have him or another licensed driver with her at all times until she got the feel of driving around in the city. He had taken her driving before but she had never driven by herself so Jake wanted to be sure his daughter was comfortable behind the wheel before he let her drive by herself. He knew she was a responsible person and that he could rely on her to go where she said she would be going and not doing anything that she was not suppose to do, but driving in Brooklyn was not like driving in the country where he learned how to drive. Mary could not wait to drive over to Cynthia's and show her friend her brand new car and Cynthia was happy for her but Mary could see that married life for Cynthia was not all she thought it would be. Mary knew that part of Cynthia's reason for getting pregnant and getting married was getting out of the house under her parents strict rules about dating and coming home on time, this way she set the rules but she did not count on a husband setting almost the same rules and a new baby who needed a lot of attention.

CHAPTER 5

In the fall of 1960 Mary went to Wharton with her father and grandmother by her side, she really did not want to stay on campus but it was paid for and it would be too much to commute and also she had a 4 year scholarship all she had to do was pay for her books. The day she moved in her father had gotten her a small television, refrigerator, Boom Box and all kinds of food for her to snack on in her room and she also had a telephone in her room so that she could keep in touch with her dad and grandma. Mary was excited when she seen all the students moving in and saying goodbye to their parents, Mary tried to hold back the tears when it was time for her dad to leave but it was just too much and so she cried and he held her and told her she would be fine this was just a new phase in her life that she was growing up but that she would always be his baby. Her grandmother told her to call as often as she wanted to and that they had no doubt that she was going to make them so proud of her. After they left Mary went up to her room and cried and cried, she was all alone her roommate had not arrived yet and she did not want to go out and meet anyone, she wanted to call Cynthia but she figured she was busy with her husband and baby and she did not want to burden her, so just laid on the bed and fell to sleep.

When Mary work up it was evening and she got up and took a walk around the dorm there were not a lot of students as far as she could tell but the campus was beautiful, lots of trees and beautiful flowers and walkways with benches for just sitting and looking, there was a nice little water fountain with a beautiful scene in back of it. Mary fell in love with the beauty of the campus and sat and just admired it for a long time. She found the commissary where there were plenty of snacks and tables and chairs for the students to just sit and talk or study whatever. Mary circled the campus and found a nice walkway for just a nice evening stroll taking in all the beauty of the place, there were rose bushes, dandelions, and tulips all around the garden area, she really fell in love with the beauty of the campus. When it began to get dark she went back to her room and read until she was tired and then went to bed. Mary said her prayers before going to bed and thank God for all that He has done in her life, she prayed for her family and especially her dad and grandma, she asked God to watch over them while she was away and keep them from all hurt, harm and danger.

The next day Mary got up early and began to separate her clothes into drawers and line up her books and her Bible. She prayed like she did every morning and wondered how she would feel about praying with an roommate in the room, she dismissed it for now and began to read her Bible, Mary especially loved the new Testament because she could relate with it so well and the old Testament had so much fighting and killing that she could not understand God putting so much violence in the Bible, it wasn't so much that she was questioning God she just could not understand it just like she could not understand all the different religions and each one claiming to be the right one that would get you into Heaven. Now that was something else she did not understand and could not make herself believe that there was only one correct religion and the rest were all wrong, why would anyone want to serve a God like that who would deliberately try to confuse his children that He clearly says he loves them all and that we all are one. Sometimes Mary would let this bother her and she never bothered to ask any questions about what she thought was confusing because if she came near to asking the answer was always that God works in mysterious ways. She could never understand serving a mysterious God but she did not have the answers and so she would just go with the flow and continue to pray and ask God for answers, she always thought that one day she would hear directly from him concerning her confusion. Mary made herself a bowl of cereal and had a banana, after breakfast she lays on her bed and read and eventually falls back to sleep, she is sleeping soundly when she hears movement in the room and looks up and see a girl looking back at her. The girl introduces herself as Mary's roommate and tells her name is Susan Andrews and reaches her hand out to take Mary's hand and Mary responds by giving Susan her hand and telling her that her name is Mary Robinson and that she is glad to meet her. Mary's roommate is a white girl and Mary is really not surprised because most of the students are white, she had seen quite a few last night. Susan's parents were with her and they introduced themselves to Mary and said they hoped that the girls got along just fine being both of the girls first time away from home. Susan got settled and said goodbye to her parents and promised to call them a little later on that evening after checking out where everything was located at on the campus. After Susan got settled and fixed of her side of the room, Mary asked her did she want to take a walk around the campus like she had done the night before. The girls walked and talked about what they thought it would be like being away from home for the first time, Mary confided in Susan that she really was a little afraid because she had been so close with her dad and told Susan that her mother had died when she was a little girl. Susan asked her was she an only child and she told her about her brother dying in Viet Nam but not anything about her missing sister or her half brothers and sisters, Mary was not comfortable talking about that part of her life with a stranger. Susan told her she was an only child and sometimes she wished she had a brother or sister to play with when she was a little girl, she said she did not want for anything she had everything she wanted and some, and that her father was a Surgeon and her mother was a housewife. She told Mary she was active in swimming and basketball and that she loved all sports but she wanted to be a doctor like her dad, she would do four years of business and them transfer to a medical facility to continue her education. The girls walked around the campus and told each other about their dreams and aspirations, Mary thanked God that she got a roommate that also had a relationship with God even though she was Catholic and Mary was Baptist, Mary did not believe in that different religion stuff anyway she believed in one God for all of us regardless of what we called Him and what our beliefs about Him were, we all believed that He is the One that controlled this Universe.

Mary met other students that she got along with she even met guys that she formed a relationship with but none that she dated, none really asked her out on a date and that was ok with her, she spoke with her dad regularly on the phone and kept him posted on what was happening in college. Her courses were strenuous but she study hard, paid attention and stayed focused, she went home sometimes on the weekends but mostly she just hung around campus and stayed to herself besides the relationship between her and her roommate. Mary eventually got a job at a restaurant not far from campus and worked a few hours a week, it really gave her spending money and she did not have to ask her dad for spending money. His job as a guard at the prison paid well but he had a lot of expenses with sending money for his other children and paying for college for her that her scholarship did not cover. He also paid her car payment and car insurance, which was expensive because of her age so she tried not to ask him for any money for extra things that she needed to take care of herself.

CHAPTER 6

Mary fell right into college life with classes, working, studying and going to church in her little red car she would also stop by and see Cynthia and the baby when she was in town. Cynthia seem to be struggling and Mary tried to get her to come back to church and maybe should would not be so depressed, but Cynthia would always tell her that she would be coming back because she missed church a lot but she never would commit to a date and Mary eventually quit asking her and stopped going by every time she was home which was mostly on the weekends. Mary loved going home on the weekends because she knew she could always get a good home cooked meal, her grandma loved cooking for her granddaughter and telling all her friends on the phone how smart her granddaughter was and how she was the first in the family to go to college. Mary also did not see her cousins that often either because not only were they Jehovah Witness but Gloria had also had a baby and was working at the hospital and did not get a lot of time to spend with her and her grandma. Mary talked to her dad a lot and he thought it was strange that she did not have a boyfriend and she told her dad she was not thinking about one either. She told Jake that between her classes and working and church she just did not have time and was not interested because they all seem to be interested in one thing and he could not believe that she was not interested in sex at all. Mary really believed in saving herself for her husband that she would have one day and did not care what anyone else said about her not being sexually active, that was something you just did not hear about in the early sixties. Mostly all the girls that she went to school with were either pregnant, had a child or two or was working some menial job in a factory or laundry somewhere and she had her sights on much higher things. Mary did wonder about Beverly her little sister sometimes because she had started to develop a sisterly love for her because she was always an only child, with her aunt Thelma it was just those two after moving away from her cousins William and Pearl and her grandparents. Although living with Aunt Thelma was different because she had Ruth and her mother Ms. Lydia whom were just like family and she had grown to love them just like family she also thought of them a lot and promised herself she would call and check on them sometime to see what Ruth was up to and her mother.

Life continued to be good for Mary and she continued to excel in her classes after the first year Mary made the Dean's List and came home and got a full time job working for Wannamaker's Department Store in the business department. Mary was responsible for the billing in the Billing Department, she was thrilled with her job and it kept her busy all summer, she did make time to go by and see Cynthia and she was pregnant again and very depressed, she confided in Mary that her husband was cheating on her and going out staying all night and coming home pushing and shoving her around. Cynthia said he was blaming her for their marriage falling apart and that it was her fault that she was pregnant again, Cynthia said he was very upset about this new baby that was due in November exactly one year from little James's birth. Mary felt so bad for Cynthia because that poor girl cried the whole time Mary was there saying her life should be going just like Mary's she should be in college somewhere instead of being bare foot and pregnant. All Mary could think to say was to tell Cynthia do not give up and pray whatever do not stop praying and believing that God would see her through this and that she would continue to pray for Cynthia. When Mary left Cynthia her heart was heavy for her friend, Cynthia's life was one Mary could never see for herself or her friend, they use to talk for hours on how they were going to go to the same college and be roommates and best friends forever. Mary broke down and cried for her friend she felt so helpless and wish there was something she could do to help the situation but she knew there was nothing she could do but pray, she could not talk to James no man wanted a female in his business and he would have just took it out on Cynthia. Mary did like she always do when things get the best of her she went and talked to her father about it and just like she knew he would advise her he told her to stay out of it, that they were married and she would wind up being the bad guy. He told her that even if Cynthia wanted to hear what she had to say she would not go against her husband whether he was wrong or right, just to keep praying like she had been and hoping it would all turn out for the best. Mary took her dad's advise and kept out of her friend's business but she made sure she called her every now and then to keep up with how her and the baby were doing. Mary also stopped by to see Mr. & Mrs. Brown they were doing fine and both of the older boys were in the armed services, they said Charles was not doing much of anything but that he did have a job and they did not see him that often. Charles was 18 and on his own and Mr. Brown did not play when you turned 18 in his household you had to be on your own. When Mary was not at work she was at home helping out her grandma around the house and still busy with church activities, all the members of her small church was always glad to see her and tell her how proud of her they were. Mary still volunteered when she had some free time and always went to see the sick and shut in and pray and sing with them, they just loved to see her coming. Before Cynthia was married she use to go with Mary all the time and they both enjoyed doing this because it would just light up the older people and especially the ones that did not have any family. Now Mary went with a group of the sisters from the church and they made sure they went it least twice a week and would take the patients communion once a month. Mary wished that she could do this all year around instead of just in the summer and holidays when she would be home on school break. Sometimes Mary would imagine her grandma being one of the patients and someone would come and minister to her like they did these patients, but Mary's grandma was different from these ladies she did not attend church but instead had friends that were like her with the card playing, drinking and smoking and dancing to jazz and blues and rock & roll. She remembered hearing songs like Blueberry Hill, Fats Dominion, Lucille, Little Richard and Sam Cooke, You Send Me, Mary does not remember hearing any gospel songs like she heard over at Cynthia's house, her family listened to the 5 Blind Boys, Clara Ward, Mahalia Jackson and the Soul Stirrers.

At the end of summer 1961 Mary was back at college and getting all settled in again. She was in a different dormitory because she was in the Honors program and she got to stay just on the outside of campus in a small apartment building that the campus owned that housed only the scholars. Her dad and grandma were just thrilled about what a great girl that Mary was turning out to be. She got a new roommate and her name was Jill Prigance and they got along well but they hardly saw each other because both of them were pretty busy with their studies and Mary had taken a full schedule and did not have time for anything but school and church. In November on the 2nd Cynthia gave birth to her daughter whom she named Carla Denise Green and she told Mary that things were much better between her and James and that he had gotten a job with the city of New York and had really settled down to being a father and husband. Mary said that she was glad for Cynthia and would stop and see her and the children over Christmas break and bring them all gifts. Mary went home for Christmas break and had a great holiday with her family, her grandma cooked all of her favorite foods just like she did for Thanksgiving and Mary got caught up on what was going on in the neighborhood which was still much the same and asked the latest about her siblings which was also pretty much the same. She learned that none of the children wanted anything to do with their father or his mother and grandma said each one of them made it very plain that was how they felt. Mary's dad had a new girlfriend and she seemed to be pretty nice, she was a nice looking woman with 2 children of her own, ages 10 and 12 and they lived in South Brooklyn both were boys. At Christmas vacation her dad introduced her to the two boys Michael 10 and Ricky 12 and their mother Ms. Anna in her late 30's. She seemed like a nice lady and the boys seemed well mannered but Mary kept her distance not so willing to share her father with anyone. Mary's dad was 48 and that was still considered a young man but not to Mary 48 seemed so old and Ms. Anna looked young anyway she did not look 30 anything and she was like 10 years younger than her dad. Mary knew enough to know that her dad needed a woman in his life she just did not think Ms. Anna was the one and she did not have a good reason for thinking that way. Mary had a very nice Christmas celebration with her family they also celebrated her dad's 48th birthday on December 27th and after all the Christmas celebration and New Year's 1962 it was back off to school starting a new year...

1962 came in with a bang, New Year's was not a big deal Mary went to church and brought in the New Year in church and it was back to the books for her. She left for school after the New Year holiday and got back into college life, she continued to study hard and concentrate on her studies. Mary did get a chance to visit Cynthia and the kids and they seemed to be doing well, Cynthia told Mary that her children were a handful being so close in age but she did get a lot of support from her mother-in-law whom she said she loved dearly because she was so supportive and did not take her son's side when they had a fight or argument. The days flew by and before Mary knew it, it was time for summer break and she was home again.

CHAPTER 7

Everything at home was basically the same, grandma still being grandma writing the numbers and cooking delicious food, and her dad still working and still having the same girlfriend Ms. Anne. Everything at church was still the same and Mary started right up with visiting the old folks and the hospitals to pray and sing with the sick and shut in. She visited Cynthia and the kids and continued to try and get her to start coming back to church but Cynthia told her she just was not ready that she had lost a lot of faith in the church and blamed them for not being more supportive when she really needed them. Mary would go by and pick Cynthia and the kids up and take them to the park and zoo and different outings that the children enjoyed and her and Cynthia would talk about old times and how much fun they had just always hanging together. Mary did not see James Sr. that often but when she did he was very cold toward her and hardly spoke, he would give her a quick hi and never bother to ask how her or her family was doing or anything about college, she thought he just did not like her but she didn't care.

Before Mary knew it summer had gone by so fast and she was back in school, still doing very well and she still had the same roommate they basically were both very busy so Mary did not see her very often. Her roommate seemed not to have much of a social life much like Mary did not have much of one. The days flew by one week after another so fast before long it was Christmas vacation again and back home with grandma and her dad. She shopped for her loved ones went to see Cynthia and the kids and dropped off presents for them. Cynthia told her things were not looking good for her and James that he was cheating on her and did not do a lot to hide the fact. Cynthia cried a lot and told her friend she could not handle this much longer she just wanted to leave everything and start over again. Mary tried to tell her that Cynthia and James should go for counseling before she broke up her family and that she was praying for her family and that Cynthia needed to talk to God and look for guidance from him. Cynthia told her she would try but she did not seem very enthused about really trying to save her marriage.

It was 1963 and Mary was back at school and she was looking forward to this being her last year. Mary continued to do very well and had the same quiet life that she had become accustomed to. She talked with her dad about what she was going to do with her life after college and she might even leave New York since her dad seemed to have gotten a new life of his own. Mary tried hard to like her dad's girlfriend but it was hard because she had become so use to it being her and her dad and she did not want to share him with anyone, even though she was away at college she was close enough for them to still be very close and they were not as close. When they went out to dinner or a movie or a basketball game Ms. Anna was right there and Mary could not stand it that they could not spend time alone like they use to. So eventually she just stopped going out with him at all she would make excuses when he called and tried to get together with her. She talked to her grandma about how she felt about Ms. Anne and her grandma told her that Ms. Anne was really a nice lady and that she loved Jacob and that Mary was just not giving her a chance. She told Mary that she did not think that Mary would think that any woman was good enough for her dad. Mary thought about what her grandma said and prayed about it and asked God to change her heart towards Ms. Anne but it did just not happen.

Part 2

Mary woke up and looked at the clock beside the bed and groaned, it had been another 3 day adventure since she had last slept in her bed or any bed for that matter. She was tired of this life she had been living for the last 5 years. Had it really been 20 longs years since she had been getting high like this, it seemed like yesterday that she had graduated from college and got that good job with IBM and was living in a beautiful apartment with all that beautiful furniture. She had moved to New York buying a gorgeous home and living a wonderful life when it all just fell apart. Mary had met her very first love at IBM where they both worked, he was tall and light brown skin and very handsome and had a great sense of humor, and Mary fell madly in love. His name was Charles Wright and he was also from New York, he was raised in the Bronx with his parents and one sister and her name was Christina and they came from a good Christian family raised up in the church. So when she met Charles and he treated her like a lady and they fell in love, Charles was the first one she had sex with and she was 25 years old. They got married in 1968 and had a son they named Antoine Charles Wright, in 1969 and he was a beautiful baby looking just like his daddy. Mary could not believe that it had been 20 years since she had gotten herself caught up in the drug world but she had made up her mind today that she was going into the hospital and once and for all get her life back together again so that she could have a relationship with her children. She knew that she could not survive if she did not get her son and baby girl back in her life, yes her and Charles broke up 1970 because he got involved with a young girl and left his family and that just devastated her because she had also lost her father to cancer that same year. She knew that she had just been feeling sorry for herself and had to make a choice today because her grandmother had threatened to have her committed the very next time she went and stayed away like this and now she had done it again. It was not like she had not tried but every time she got her check it seemed like that crack would be calling her name or some cracked-up friend would call and tell her how much money they had toward a bag and just like that she would be gone on a mission as they called it in the drug world. Charles had taken Antoine off of her a long time ago and raised him when she first started getting all caught in drugs before crack was even around. She started with marijuana with Charles before they were married, it was the cool thing to do and she wanted to do whatever her husband was doing and she really liked the way it relaxed her with taking care of Antoine while Charles worked. Mary did have her own car and she would go and see her grandma back on 18th Street she still was not on speaking terms with her father. She had fallen out with her father over something that had to do with Ms. Anne who had told her father that she was getting high. It was now 1995 and she was back living with her grandma after a second marriage had failed because of her drug use. Her second marriage happen to be with another Charles, Cynthia's baby brother, she had run into him at a friends house with whom she would hang out, she was on her way into her friend's house and Charles walked up to her and said "hi Mary, do you remember me I am Cynthia's baby brother Charles" and he put a marijuana joint into her hand and Mary immediately remembered him. Mary and Charles started dating and she asked about Cynthia and was told that Cynthia had gotten a divorce from James and was now married again to a guy name Dennis and they were in the church and Cynthia had another son, they were living in California and was doing well. She asked about her God children and Charles told her that he did not see them often because they were with their dad who had raised them and as far as he knew they were both doing well, now this was 1970. Mary and Charles had lived together for a couple of years and then they broke up it was on both of them, Mary was not quite ready to settle down because she had been so sheltered and neither was Charles. Mary had started going out with her friends to bars and smoking weed and drinking and she really liked that freedom and living with Charles was like being married again and she did not want any parts of that so they went their separate ways. Mary began working for an Electric Company in their Business Department and was making very good money and had a nice apartment in South Brooklyn. Now all these thoughts began to run around in her head as she contemplated going into rehab again, she had tried this rehab thing three other times and every time it would last for a few months and she would relapse. Mary thought if she could just follow the program she could whip this thing she had seen countless people do it one of which was her husband Charles they had gotten back together in 1975 and gotten married after staying apart for three years and had a son Charles Junior born on July 28, 1978 and Mary was in Heaven, Charles got a good job with the city and rose up in the ranks very quickly and Mary herself went back to the Electric Company and so they bought a beautiful home in South Brooklyn and everything was fine until Charles introduced her to crack cocaine in 1982 and the drug was everywhere. She had tried rehab when Charles got clean in 1990 but she could not stay clean and he just refused to stay with her because he was in a program called Narcotics Anonymous and they advised him if he wanted to stay clean he was going to have stay away from her and eventually he took their advice and got custody of his children. So here she was again it was 1992 and she still could not get it together even to get her family back why did it seem like such a struggle when she knew it could be done but it was not easy so she struggled with making the call and she had promised her grandma who was 98 and still living in her home and taking care of herself and in her right mind. Her grandma knew about marijuana but she did not know anything about this crack stuff she could not understand how Mary could let herself get caught up with such foolishness as she called it. She would tell Mary to just stop it what was the big deal, she told her many times that your dad is turning over in his grave to see what a mess you have made of your life. Mary hated to hear her talk about her dad because there was so much guilt there about how she just would not have anything to do with him until he was diagnosed with cancer back in 1985 and was given three months to live and he died 3 months after he was diagnosed on September 22, 1985 and Mary was truly devastated she really struggled with she only had 3 months to beg her father forgiveness for being such a stubborn fool and her grandma was 90 years old and had to bury her child. Mary hated these thoughts and wish she could go back and change things, she also wished she could kick this drug habit which had just taken over her whole life and had given her nothing but grief. Mary hated when she thought like this it always made her head hurt and she would pick up the phone at least 50 times and set it down again. Mary got on her knees and prayed as she had done so many times before but she just had to get it right and so she prayed for guidance and for God to take away obsession and compulsion to use. Mary got up off her knees and made the phone call to the drug abuse center, she held the phone and did not say anything when the voice on the other end said "Hello Gateway Rehabilitation Center may I help you?" Mary froze, the voice on the other end said "Gateway can I help you", Mary blurted out, "I need help bad can I please talk with someone regarding admittance"? The voice on the other end said "of course have you ever been here before", Mary said yes and she was asked did she remember her counselor's name and what was her drug of choice, Mary told the lady her name and said her drug of choice was crack cocaine and just as she said that the beep came across letting her know there was another call. Mary would not answer the other call knowing it was either Charles wanting to know if she had made the call or one of her crack buddies ready to go out and get their day started by hustling for money by any means necessary to get their crack. Mary remembered the counselor's name was Ms. Davis and told the lady on the other end of the phone to just ignore the beep because it was not important. The lady asked her to hold on while she punched in the information on the computer. She came back on the phone and told Mary that she had a bed and how fast could she get there. Mary told the lady that she did not have a dime and did not know anyone that would trust her, she said maybe she could at least get carfare there maybe she could ask her grandma but her grandma had stopped giving her anything and she had even stolen things out of the house. She asked the lady to hold the phone while she checked with grandma, when she told her grandma what she wanted it for her grandma insisted on talking with the lady to verify Mary's story. When her grandma got on the phone and the lady explained to her that Mary had agreed to come into rehab and that they were expecting her, grandma told the lady she would give Mary just enough for carfare and not a dime more because she was just fed up with her. She told the lady that she was 90 years old and she had all she could take of Mary and this drug thing, she began to tell the lady all that Mary had thrown away on this drug mess and she was not going to let Mary be the death of her. Mary told the lady she was on her way after her grandma gave her the carfare and a very good ear beating to go along with it. After Mary left home she went straight to the bus stop and she was very careful to stay clear of all the known crack corners. While Mary was waiting for the bus a car drove up with 4 crack heads on their way to the crack house, they asked Mary where she was on her way to and at first Mary would not tell them where she was on her way to and refused to get into the car. Someone in the back of the car pull out a small baggie with crack in it and told her he would share with her and he also had a pocketful of money, the other guys did not have any money or drugs and they knew if Mary came along this fool in the back seat would spend all his money. They began to tell Mary to come on they would all have a nice time she knew that she would have to have sex with the guy with the money but she also knew that she became very weak just seeing those drugs and all thoughts of rehab were off. Into the back seat Mary went and off to the crack house they went. Mary stayed all night and got high with the fellows and had sex with all of them and spent all of the one guy's money which was about $400 plus the crack he had already had with him. By the time they were finished with her and she had begged for all the crack that anyone would give her it was the next day and she had not seen her grandma in 4 days. Mary was sick and feeling very low, she needed some more crack and did not want to think of going into rehab, she just wanted one more hit and then she would go to rehab. She went home and her grandma let her in, she was desperate, her grandma looked at her and just turned and walked into the kitchen. Mary looked at the VCR and she had never stolen anything off her grandma but money before, she thought of her grandma and her husband and son but the thought did not last long because she thought of the pipe and she unhooked the VCR and left. Mary stayed for another night selling her body for crack and then she went home late at night knowing that she would have to wake her grandma up to get in but she was just so tired what grandma would say would go in one ear and out the other she just wanted to rest. When Mary rang the bell and waited for her grandma to open up the door instead Uncle Johnny opened the door and said come right on in young lady, Mary froze because her uncle was very quiet and never got involved in family affairs unless it was his children. She went into the living room and there was her aunts Evelyn and Nora and Evelyn spoke first, she told Mary that the family had all they were going to take from her treating their 90 year old mother like dirt, stealing what little she had and they were fed up. Mary began to cry and asked for another chance, that she was willing to go into rehab for 30 days and try again. Her uncle told her that did not work before and that she was killing their mom, and she only had one choice a long term treatment center and they had checked one out that was 50 miles from Brooklyn and it was on a farm and it had a very good record of long term recovery. Her uncle told her it was a two year program and she could not think of coming home for 2 years and that he was prepared to take her now, meantime Grandma Irene was crying up a storm and her daughters kept telling her that it was for the best otherwise she would never get it together. It was late but Mary asked them could she please talk to Charles and tell him what was going on, they said he knew but that she could call him. When Mary got Charles on the phone she just broke down and told him how sorry she was and that she loved him and her son and was going to get better this time. Charles told Mary that he loved her also and would be waiting for her when she got herself well again.

Part 3

When Mary and her uncle Johnny got to the rehab facility it was 5 am and there was only a porch light on another light in hallway on. The lady that let them in took them into her office and introduced herself as Ms. Zilch and explained the program to Mary and her uncle, she explained that Mary's husband's insurance would cover the whole bill and that it was a two year program the date was April 3, 1993. Mary was taken to detox and locked into a room by herself and Ms. Zilch told her to try and get some rest, Mary was devastated and laid on the bed and just cried she knew that she would be sick once the crack was all out of her body. When Mary woke up the next morning she was beginning to feel sick and when Ms. Zilch came in and asked how she was feeling she told her sick and Ms. Zilch gave her some medication and told her she would probably sleep for awhile. When Mary woke again it was dark outside, she asked for something to drink because her throat was so dry and Mary went back to sleep, she slept for 2 days and on the third day Ms. Zilch told her she would have to get up and talk to her counselor and nurse who would access her and put her on prescribed medication to help deal with the pain and nauseated feeling she was going to be feeling for a few days. Mary stayed in her room for two weeks feeling awful; Ms. Zilch tried talking to her but to no avail she finally told Mary that she would have to start doing what was required of her that was part of the deal in her coming to their facility. She assigned Mary a counselor and told her that she would have to come out of her room that she would no longer be assigned to that room but that she would be assigned to another room and would have a roommate. Mary was taken to meet her new counselor Ms. Philips and was told what the policy and procedures were for the facility, she had her two weeks to get over the sick feeling of being without crack in her system and now she would have to start to rehabilitate. Mary just sat and listened, she was given papers to sign and list of the policies and procedures of what was and was not allowed in the two years that this would be her home. Mary could not even image being in this place for another day and two years was too much for the imagination, she thought of leaving this place but for one thing it was on a farm and very far from the city and the rehab had a policy that they would not take you back you had to get someone to come and get you and Mary knew that would not happen. Her family had already told her that she would have to stay for the 2 years because they had tried everything else and this was her last shot. So Mary settled down and was introduced to her roommate who had already been there a year, they wanted the newcomer to be with someone that had spent some time in the facility and was having a very good record of what to do to graduate from this facility and get started on a new way of life. Her new roommate was a black girl and her name was Jennifer Smith and she was also from New York there were people there from all over the United States. The facility was well known for its success rate and they again wanted Mary with someone that was familiar with where Mary was from. Mary was assigned kitchen duty and later that afternoon her new roommate Jennifer would take her around and show her the facility. Ms. Philips told Mary that no one was going to babysit her and she did not have to run away she was not court appointed there like some of the residents and could leave on her own free will whenever she wanted to. Mary knew this but she was just so upset with herself every time she thought of how far she had fell from grace it was hard to believe that she had come this far down in 8 years and what a struggle it was just to try and get back up she knew that time was running out and that Charles would not continue to wait for her to get herself together when he had gotten himself clean and have been clean for 5 years and has been raising their son all by himself and doing a good job. Anthony had already taken Antoine out of her life as soon as she got strung out on drugs, Mary did not want to lose both of her boys, they were her life and she knew she had to do it for them and for herself, she vowed to stick it out.

Ms. Philips took Mary to her intake room to get her things and show her where her room with Jennifer was going to be and after Mary got her things and set up her side of the room, her and Jennifer went around to check out the facility. Jennifer showed Mary what a beautiful place it was and told Mary that after she earned points she would be going out on the van with the other girls to visit other facilities, go shopping and also go to meetings. She explained to Mary that meetings were a requirement and that they attended group sessions everyday and had charts on how their progress was coming, she also told Mary that most of the people that came to this facility stayed and that most of them became productive members of society and stayed clean. She explained that it was a 12 step program that followed the example of Narcotics Anonymous the program that Charles was still a member of. Jennifer took Mary around and introduced her to the other girls and showed her around the facility, the outside was beautiful with flower garden and beautiful landscape very well taken care of and Jennifer told her that guys from the other facility would maintain the lawn, she also explained that they had dances some times and the guys would come to their facility or they would go to theirs and that they were never left alone with the guys. The facility number one rule was no relationships while still in rehab and if anyone broke that rule they would be put out of the facility, the guy's facility ran just like the girls same strict rules. After showing Mary all around the place which housed about 50 people they went back to their rooms to talk for awhile before dinner. That was another strict rule not too much time in your rooms the facility wanted the girls to be actively working on their recovery not locked up in their rooms so they were kept quite busy all week long. The weekends were for families coming up to visit loved ones and going to church on Sundays, the church of your choice they had a Baptist, Catholic, Methodist and Presbyterian churches that the van would take the girls to if they wanted to go and Mary said that she thought she would be interested in that, although it would be a few weeks before she was allowed to go anywhere. Dinner was served at 5:30 and the kitchen was cleaned up and then they went to their rooms until 7pm where they either went out to a meeting or went to meetings at the facility but Mary was not required to do either she could go back to her room and she would start the program the following day.

The next day started off with meds the first thing in the morning after showers and the making up of beds and then breakfast. Mary was shown downstairs to where she would help prepare and serve breakfast and dinner as her job duties, every resident had a specific job that she was required to do. Mary was called into her counselor's office after breakfast and Ms. Philips gave her papers to fill out and wanted to talk with her about her drug of choice and her family and what she wanted out of the program. Mary talked about her son's and their fathers, about her grandma and about her beloved father and how when he got sick that she was upset with him because of his girlfriend and that was part of the reason she turned to hard drugs. She said before then she had only smoked weed as a recreational thing that she done with her husband Anthony, before then she had never even had a beer of a drink because she was never interested in either. She talked about being active in the church and how she loved going to church until she met Anthony at her job and began to date him, she said Anthony was her very first boyfriend and he was the first one she had sex with at the age of 25. Ms. Philips could hardly hold back the shock look she gave to Mary when Mary told her that she was a virgin until she met her husband 1967, she told Mary that she did not know of any 25 year old virgins in her lifetime. Mary felt comfortable talking with Ms. Philips so she began to tell her all about her early childhood when she was taken to Georgia by her mother and left until her father came and got her at the age of 15. She told her what a struggle life has been starting at such a young age for her then seeming to get so much better during her college years and even after her first marriage then struggling again when things went bad between her and her dad, then the divorce and finally the drugs. Mary said things were good again when she married Charles and had her second child with him three years later her beloved daughter, she just knew that everything would be fine and all her struggles were behind her, Mary did not think anything could take away the joy and love she had for her new family but now she had sunk so far and did not know how it happened so fast. Mary just wanted to know when would it get better and if it ever would, losing her children out of her life was just the ultimate there would be no reason to go on she told Ms. Philips if she could not get them back in her life. They talked a little while longer and Ms. Philips told Mary that she would keep close contact with her and try and do all she could do with the help of the facility to get her back on the right track and a renewed relationship with her sons. Mary went back to her room, her roommate was at a meeting for the evening so she picked up some literature she seen laying around and read for a little bit, some of it was familiar because she had supported Charles in his recovery but could never get it for herself. A couple of days here and there but never any amount of substantial time but Charles refused to leave his wife even though the N.A. program and his sponsor advised him that Mary would only send him back out in the streets, but Mary was the one to leave him and go back to her grandma's. After reading a little Mary got down on her knees and prayed like she had never prayed before, she talked to God and asked for another chance to get it right, Mary told the Lord that she knew she could not do this without him and promised Him that if He would bring her up out of this she would never leave Him again. Mary got her evening meds and came back and laid down and just laid awake praying and thinking about her family until she finally drifted off to sleep and slept the most peaceful sleep she had in years.

The next morning Mary was woke by a buzzer that went off in the hallways letting everyone know it was time to get up and get their day started. Mary showered and got dressed and went into the cafeteria for breakfast, breakfast was eggs, bacon, toast, fruit and juice and coffer or tea. After breakfast it was meds, you got in line for that and all the girls had a schedule for the month of what activities they would follow for each day and Mary was also given one. So day one went like this, group and everyone in that group with a group leader would go into their group and each person was required to go around in the circle introducing themselves and start with a topic they wanted to hear or if there was a new person like Mary she was asked to say her name and that she was an addict and say something about herself. Mary was reluctant at first but thought about her prayer and knew that she was not going to be stubborn like she knew she could get and try very hard to do this thing the right way. So she said "Hi my name is Mary and I am an addict" wow that was hard and it took a lot of courage to say it on the first day in group. They went around the circle and then everyone would share where they were at in their recovery program, some had issues that were devastating like HIV positive and Hepatics.C and liver diseases also life threatening sickness from their active drug use. Mary had her complete physical when she came into the facility and all her test results came back negative, she began to thank God right then and there that she was spared from having any of these diseases. Although she had never shot heroin she had a lot of unprotected sex and just the thought of a needle sent her into orbit, Mary has always been deathly afraid of needles, she did try other drugs but never heroin and never shooting up anything that was just out. After group it was time for chores which everyone was assigned to some kind of chore daily. Mary was working in the kitchen which she liked, it consisted of cooking, preparing the meals, serving and cleaning then it was time for one on one with your counselor after that there were girls there that had their children with them so they had time with their children. When it was time for meetings and going out of the building for meetings or shopping for the facility then other girls would be assigned the babysitting duty of watching other's children, only ladies with children had to babysit. After all of this was accomplished then the ladies would have a little down time and they were allowed to watch a hour of television only selected channels that the staff approved of, no violence and music just like game shows and discussion about relevant subjects such as church positive subjects. Mary's first one on one with her counselor proved to be very beneficial to Mary because she found that it very easy to talk with Ms. Philips and felt that Ms. Philips really cared so the next one on one Ms. Philips told her that she would have to write a drug history and share it with Ms. Philips and with the group, she was told that she was to go back to the very first time she tried a drink or a drug and come up to the present.

The next day after her chores and group were done and it was down time Mary began to think back to the first time she took a hit off of a joint and so Mary began to write, She started with meeting her first husband at her job and how he pursued her, Anthony would say nice things but Mary could see the way he looked at her body that he had other things on his mind so she stayed clear of him but he was insistent and started asking her to go to lunch with him but she would always say no she had never been on a date and she was 24, It was not that she was afraid of men she just was not interested in Anthony or any other guy for that matter, the difference was she saw Anthony everyday and he was the only black man that worked in her office and he was handsome. On Valentine Day that year he sent her a dozen roses with a note so beautiful she shared it with some of the girls in the office and they could not believe that she continued to turn him down. The note read roses are red, violets are blue I wish somehow it could be me and you and he signed it and drew a lot roses around a heart. Mary was touched and she knew she had to respond by this time she had another girlfriend since graduating from college that she was close with and she had been telling her about Anthony, so she called her and her friend asked her was she crazy or gay what was wrong with a date. Mary thought about it and went to lunch with Anthony on Valentine's Day and all she could think was he is really a gentleman and knew how to treat a lady, he opened the doors for her, he told her how she was different from any girl he had every met and he swept

Mary off her feet. They went out everyday in the month of February, out to dinner and a movie and then Anthony wanted Mary to come up to his apartment, but she refused that is where she drew the line because she knew what was next. So the next few days they dated and Anthony took her up to his apartment and it was about three weeks before she even let Anthony kiss her and he was absolutely shocked that she had never French kiss before, Mary told him that she only kissed one boy before years ago and his name was Charles and it was her best friend's brother and they called themselves going together and he never got fresh with her no heavy petting and none of that open mouth stuff, she thought that was just awful. Anthony could not believe that Mary was a 25 year old virgin, it just was not heard of in this day and age but he respected her for it and did not push the issue he told her only when she thought she was ready but it was getting hard to be around her and not want to have sex with her. So a few days later Mary was back up Anthony's apartment and Mary and Anthony began kissing and it led to heavy petting and Mary started backing off saying no, and Anthony started to become frustrated because he would always leave with an erection so he told Mary they would have to stop seeing each other because just becoming too much pressure. Anthony told Mary that he was a man with a man's desires and he understood that Mary wanted to wait until her wedding night and he always told her that they would one day get married but they were not even engaged yet and just could not go on like this. Mary thought it was really too soon to even be talking about marriage because they had just started dating and did not really know each other. Mary tried to think about being without Anthony she had never had a relationship with anyone like this before and she was really crazy about Anthony so instead of saying no to him Mary said yes she did not want to take a chance of losing him he told her that they he would just hold her in his arms and talk about it without any kissing and petting and if she still did not want to go through with having sex he would just drop it. Well after thinking about it for a little while and lying in his arms Mary started thinking she wanted to please her man so she said yes, because she was afraid of losing him, there was nothing to talk about she just wanted to do it. Well Anthony was all over her and telling her that she was the only one for him and that he had never felt this way before and that he would be very gentle with her and not hurt her.. Well Mary said how she weakened under his touch and he kept pulling her underwear down and saying that he was not going to penetrate her but he did and he did try to be gentle but it still hurt and Mary was bleeding. Mary felt terrible because she really wanted to save herself for her husband and Anthony kept telling her he was going to be her husband but she could not stop crying and Anthony said she made him feel like he had raped her and he felt awful and so he cried also. They continued to see each other and started having protective sex and it did not hurt like it did the first time, Mary made sure that they had safe sex she did not want to become pregnant but that was not the case, it was a little late for protection because Mary got pregnant after the first time having sex with Anthony. Anthony did not want to get married right now because he thought they were not prepared for a family now and Mary out right refused to have an abortion, she would not put that on her conscience. So they went to Anthony's family and talked with them and his parents told him the right thing to do was to get married and that they loved each other and that they could make it work. Mary and Anthony then went to Jake and Grandma Irene and told them that she was pregnant and that her and Anthony were planning on getting married, they were not very upset after all Mary was 25 and her and Anthony were in love.

Well the baby was due in November so Anthony and Mary had to have an apartment big enough for the baby and so they made plans to get married in June, so on June 6, 1968 at Anthony's parent's house they got married and had a small reception for friends and family. Mary took a leave of absence from her job when she was 6 months pregnant and started getting ready for the baby which was due in November, married life seemed great she was so much in love with Anthony and he seemed to be in love with her, but sometimes she seemed to think that Anthony was not as happy about this marriage and expecting baby as she was. Her son was born on November 28, 1968 and named Antoine Charles Wright, Charles did not want a junior and Mary never asked why.

Mary had to get to the part about her first drink and drug, that happened when they were together at a New Year's Eve party that friends of Anthony was given. They were sitting around after Charles had made introductions and everyone was drinking and laughing after the New Year came in and they were wishing everyone a Happy 1969 and toasting each other. Anthony gave Mary a small glass of wine so that she could toast with everyone else and her and Anthony kissed and brought in the New Year, This was 1969 and Mary could not have been happier, she had never really partied before the few Christians she hung around with did not go in for that secular music and stuff and she knew it was because of Anthony that she was so happy. Mary noticed almost everyone passing a cigarette around taking a drag pass it on and when it got to Anthony he also took a drag off of it and handed to her and told her to do the same, Mary told him no she did not smoke and did not want to, but Anthony told her just a little puff would not hurt her and so she did. Mary felt very light headed and felt as if she was floating, she liked the feeling right away and Anthony told her he only done it on occasions like birthday parties, and other celebrations. They had a good time and stayed late and she smoked a little more and when they went home they made love and it seemed the like it was the best ever and Anthony told her that marijuana was the cause of that feeling.

Anthony was still working and Mary was staying home being the housewife and taking care of her son. Anthony would bring home some weed every once in a while and he and Mary would get high together, Mary loved him so much she would do anything for him and he seemed to love her but he started staying later and later at the office and would get real nasty with her when she questioned him. Then Mary started smoking every weekend and drinking wine because she was lonely and Anthony was staying away more and more. Then one night in late spring he stayed out all night and when Mary said she questioned him he got angry at her and told her to leave him alone that she forced him into the marriage thing. Mary was stunned this is the first she heard that he was upset with her for getting pregnant, like she did it on purpose. That night Anthony slept in the guest room and starting acting very different toward her, he was the same with the baby, he loved little Antoine as they called him but his feelings toward his wife seem to change overnight. At first it was a night here and there, then it got to be every weekend, then it got to be the whole weekend and he came home on the weekdays and Mary could not say one word about him staying out all weekend or he would fight with her. Mary had no one she could talk to she was not going to tell her father or grandma and she had no close friends, by this time in her life Cynthia had broken up with her husband and left him and the kids and got a new guy she married and they moved to California. Mary felt like there was a hole in her heart, it just hurt so bad and there just seemed to be nothing she could do about that empty feeling. Mary cried a lot and tried to smother her baby with love, she took him to the park, and zoo and all kinds of outdoor activities and played with him and took good care of him, Anthony was not even talking with her, and he had a life of his own. One day he just told her he wanted a divorce he had someone else and he also wanted to take Antoine, Mary screamed and hollered and told him over her dead body, he could leave but he could not take her baby, she even begged him for them to try counseling so they could save their marriage, he told her there was nothing to save and he would take her to court over Antoine because he could provide a better life for him, she did not even have a job he said. Mary lost her husband and son it was too big of a battle to fight, his parents had money his father was a surgeon and his mom did not work and Antoine was their only grandchild and they got a good attorney and won. Mary's dad said that he would have gotten an attorney and fought for his grandson stating that a child belong with their mother, Mary was hurt and said hurtful words telling her dad "yea just like I was with my mom." Things went straight downhill for Mary after that she got some new friends, a new job working in the business office of the Transit System and began going out to bars drinking and smoking weed and she had even started drinking cough syrup for the codeine in it. Mary began going to a psychologist who then referred her to a psychiatrist because she was very depressed and so he described her pills and she just stayed high all the time. Mary was smoking weed around the clock, she would smoke before work in the morning, come out on her lunch with some of her friends and they would go to a secluded spot in the park and smoke on her lunch break. Mary was good at her job so no one knew what was going on. She could not see her son because Anthony told the authorities that she was getting high all the time and was not a good example for their son, so Mary's son did not know his mother because he was only a baby when this happened. She could not believe she was doing to her child what was done to her whether it was willingly or not, she tried a few times to stop getting high on her own but it never worked. So when Mary met Charles she was getting high on weed and cough syrup, she was not drinking alcohol she only did a little wine because anything stronger would have her so out of it she did not know what happened to her while she was drunk. Onetime she got drunk with one of her friends and drove home drunk and some guy she knew was in her apartment when she woke up off the couch, she knew him and liked him but did not know how he got in her apartment and he said he got in by some guy that had followed her home and must have snuck in her apartment because he said her keys were on the floor when he knocked on her door and this strange guy just opened the door and walked out and he said Mary was on the couch knocked out with all her clothes on so he just stayed in case the guy would come back. That was it for the drinking with Mary she did not like it anyway because she could not hold her liquor and would be driving around drunk and sick as a dog the next morning and further more she did not like the taste, so she just left it alone and stuck with cough syrup and weed. The cough syrup that her and her friends would get they would just go into the store and get it off the shelf, until they made it so you needed a prescription to get it because of the codeine. Mary and her friends went through all kinds of changes to get the cough syrup even going to the doctor's office and stealing a whole pad when he turned his head and began to write the prescriptions for it themselves. Mary and her friends found out about a lady that use to get it by the gallons and started selling them half pints and pints and boy were they in their world. They would get cough syrup and all go to Mary's apartment because she was the only one that did not have any kids so they would sit and listen to jazz and nod all night just like they had taken heroin.

Mary really went wild after her husband stopped all contact with her and Antoine and got a divorce citing irreconcilable differences. Anthony stated in the custody battle that Mary was addicted to all kinds of pills and drugs and he did not want his son around her unless she could clean up her act and the courts sided with him and it was truly downhill with the getting high all the time until Mary ran into Charles again. At first Mary was just using Charles to get over Anthony she was not interested in him at all Anthony had really taken her heart and tore it to pieces and she did not want the pieces put back together again it was just too painful. Mary was tired of struggling in her life it just seemed like she was doomed for failure and she just wanted to stay high and never come down, but Charles was determined he really like Mary and all her friends knew that he really like her and kept telling her to give him a chance. Charles was a nice young man he did not have any children but he did smoke a lot of weed and drink also and that is why Mary was interested in him at all because he kept weed and it was the good weed. Before Charles came into her life Mary was just wild, hanging in bars all the time, she stayed high, going with married men two and three different ones at the same time she just did not care. Mary did not want to ever love again it just hurt too much she felt like playing around was just great no commitments and that's how she wanted it. When she looks back it was just a blessing that she did not get hurt while out there in the streets, New York was a dangerous place especially the places she went around and this was the time of the Black Panthers and hippies and the heroin scene was even getting bigger around this time. They had riots earlier in 1968 when Martin Luther King got killed and also when Malcolm got killed things were very tense around New York because they had a lot of Muslims in New York. Mary strung Charles along for awhile and kept him at a distance, but he was persistent and when they were in the bar together he would always play a song by the Temptations called "I Can't Get Next To You" and Mary liked that song also because she loved the Temptations and mostly anything that Motown put out. Mary and Charles continued to see each other for a while longer but eventually they went their separate ways and did not run into each other again until 1975 and Mary had settled down some still smoking weed and drinking a little white wine and Charles was still doing the same thing, he told her he had left New York for a while and was living with some girl in Chicago but that did not work out because after a while the girl started liking women so he came back to New York. They really started seeing each other seriously and it was just them two, Charles did not want to lose Mary again so he purposed to her and she said yes. Mary took Charles to meet her dad and he asked Jacob for Mary's hand in marriage, Jacob liked Charles right away and they got along real well, they even went fishing and hunting together and Charles liked Jacob. Charles even met Grandma Irene and she fell right in love with him, he was not like Anthony and none of Mary's family liked Anthony and his family because his family thought they were better and they did not let them see Antoine, they said because Mary was a bad influence on Antoine. So Mary's grandma and dad loved them some Charles, he was so respectful and would do anything for Grandma Irene or Jacob who was still with his Ms. Anna and after Mary had the baby Jacob wanted to be a part of his daughter's new family. Things were never like they use to be but at least Mary was on speaking terms with her father again. Charles knew all about Mary's issues with depression, smoking weed and running around with married men but he just put it all behind them and wanted to start fresh. Charles's family did not feel the same way about Mary, his oldest brother James knew Mary from the streets and told his family that Charles could do a lot better than Mary. Charles's mother Mrs. Brown was surprised because she knew Mary from church and when Mary and Cynthia were best friends and how she use to wish that Cynthia was more like Mary because everyone loved Mary and she was a Christian. But she listened to what her son said and she did not want Charles to marry Mary, she refused to go to the wedding which was held on November 22, 1975 and James and his wife were the only ones on Charles's side of the family to come, even Cynthia refused to come. Mary was alright with the way their were feeling because by this time she was really started to love Charles and thoughts of Anthony and ever loving him were gone, however her baby was another thing it was 1975 and he was 7 years old and did not know anything about his mother. Mary began to pray to God to let her have a relationship with her son but his attorney told Anthony as long as she smoked weed he could legally keep her away and so she prayed to be able to get rid of the addiction and it was not easy. Mary still had her job and Charles had his job and they got an apartment in West Brooklyn, Mary let all of her old friends go and started going back to church, all the church members were glad to see her return and her and Mrs. Brown started getting along with each other again after Mrs. Brown seen Mary trying to change her life around. Mary started going to church with her sister-in-law Vonnie, James's wife but their life style's were different because Mary could not give up the weed and she was still prescribed some pills for her nerves and Vonnie had 4 children and a job as a school teacher that kept her busy. She was not like Mary she did not get high with her husband like Mary did, Mary, Charles and James regularly went to the bar and smoked weed all the time. At first James and Mary did not get along but James seen how his baby brother loved her and after getting to know her he fell in love with her also. Mary was just a regular person she was not stuck up like James thought she was because he hardly remembered her being friends with his sister because he was away in the army when Mary and Cynthia were good friends so had to find out for himself.

The first two years of their marriage was kind of hectic because Charles started going out with his friends and leaving Mary at home which she was not going to have any of that. Mary knew exactly where that would lead and she refused to have any part of it, when Charles went out hanging and she thought he might be messing around she went out and done the same thing, she knew it was not the right thing to do but she promised herself she would never be caught off guard again, if Charles thought he was going to mess around and keep his family together he had another thought coming. Then Mary got pregnant and Charles was absolutely thrilled at the thought of a baby, they became closer and Mary knew that she had started loving Charles unconditionally and the feelings were mutual on Charles's end.

On July 28, 1978 they welcomed Charles Matthew Brown Jr. into the world; he weighed 7lb 15 oz and was a beautiful baby. Charles loved being a father and Mary was just ecstatic

God had given her another chance to do it right, although Mary did not stop smoking weed when she got pregnant she did stop once her baby was born because she was breast feeding him for a while but the baby was so greedy that she did not have enough milk for him and had to put him on formula also. After the baby was born she made up her mind to stop with the weed and try to get to see her oldest son who was 10 now and did not know his mother at all. Charles had remarried and Antoine was calling her mom she guessed, she did not know but they got an attorney and Mary was granted supervised visits which she did not like at all. Her son did not know her so Mary began to tell Antoine about how she lost custody of him and how her life just spiral downhill after she lost her family. Antoine was a smart child and he did understand but he still did not know her and he told his mom that he called Ms Cynthia by her name and he called his grandma "mom" that was the only mother he knew because he was 2 when they got divorced and so he had heard about his real mother but was told she was too sick to see him. He told his mom that he had never called Ms. Cynthia (his stepmom) anything but Ms. Cynthia. Eventually as long as Mary stayed clean she could get her son every other weekend and Antoine loved coming over and playing with his baby brother CJ and Mary stayed clean and got pregnant again and had a baby girl on May 8, 1981 when Mary was 38 years old. Mary got her tubes tied because she had the perfect family she had her beautiful daughter whom they named Lynnet Brown and the boys were just static over her. Everything was going so good in Mary's life she was truly in love with her husband and children and they had wonderful times together and as the children got older they would go on week vacations together. Charles let Mary take Antoine and it was just one big happy family and then Mary's father got diagnosed with lung cancer and was given 6 months to live and then things came crashing down for her. Mary took her father for his treatments, he went to church with her and Mary even became close with Ms. Anna who stood right beside Jacob to the end. It was so sad to see her father go down like that from the chemo and radiation, he lost so much weight and when they could do no more for him they let the family know and Jacob went home to die. Mary and Grandma Irene took it so hard it just devastated Mary to see her frail grandma cry for her child like that, after he died it seemed like Mary was in a fog, she don't remember the wake, funeral burial or anything about that time. Charles and his mother had to take over the care of her children, Net was still a baby a little over 1 and Mary went to the doctor's to get something just to get her through this depression of losing her father and in no time she was back to using marijuana and taking pills. Charles tried to understand what she was going through but it was a bit much for him with working and taking care of the children that he started using again himself. One day he came home with a pipe with some crack in it and told Mary to try it he said it was something new and would get you so high you would not want anything else. Well Mary tried and told Charles she did not feel anything, she tried again same results. He told her she was not inhaling it right and tried to show her but she got fed up and just said she would stick with the weed it worked. Well Charles kept trying it and eventually he kept at Mary for them to try it together and she finally got that feeling that Charles was talking about. It took off from there and she just got more and more into it and did not want to do anything else, she began to neglect the kids and Anthony found out and stopped Antoine from visiting her. Her and Charles almost lost everything, Charles's mother stepped in and took CJ and Net and told Charles that he would lose everything including his life if he did not get himself together and get his family together. Crack had started to get real bad around the neighborhood and Charles almost lost his job, Mary had not went back to work after having Net because she thought Net was too young for babysitters. In 1984 Charles's job gave him an ultimate either get himself together or lose his job and his pension and all of his benefits. They told him he had to go into a program for 6 months and his job would be waiting and he would get sick pay until he returned to work. He could not worry about Mary he had to get his priorities together and they were his children and so in 1984 he went into rehab and worked the program and came out and tried to work with his wife even though they told him at the program that was dangerous for his recovery he did it anyway. It proved to be a mistake because Mary started going out staying all night getting high coming back a day or two later declaring that it was the last time. After a while Charles just told her to leave and go stay with her grandma until she decided what she wanted to do with the rest of her life because he was not going to subject his children to a life of crack cocaine from their mother. After that Mary said she just continued going down hill and could not find her way back.

Mary finished her history of drug use and started working the program she worked, went to meetings, shared where she was in her recovery and looked forward to the visits from her family. Mary did worry about her grandma because she could not see her and only talked to her on the phone, although Charles told her he was taking good care of her and had help come in 3 to 4 times week to clean and do things that Grandma Irene needed done. Grandma Irene was still real sharp and still played her numbers but Charles stopped her from selling liquor and beer because the neighborhood was becoming very bad with the crack epidemic and he did not want those crack heads to run in there on Grandma Irene. He also had some neighborhood friends that he knew were good people check on her from time to time while he was busy with work and his children. Both of the children were doing great in school and Antoine was also doing well, all Charles kept reminding Mary was that she had 1 more year to do and they would be back together and move into a real nice neighborhood where they could raise their children. While in rehab Mary learned a lot about herself why she got high it was not the drug by itself that was only 10 percent of the problem the other 90 was her and what she had to deal with in her life and instead of facing the pain, going through the pain to get to the other side she chose to numb the pain with drugs. She was also taught how she had to make amends to people she had harmed in her addiction; she learned that making amends was for her and not for the other person. She had to let go of all the hurt and pain and give it to God. She also learned that she had to get a God of her understanding and at first she did not understand this because she always thought there was just one God no matter what your beliefs but through meetings and sharing she got to understand that not everybody came into recovery understanding anything about God at all. Mary did have the advantage of an earlier relationship with God and that did help but it was so much deeper than that. After 1 ½ years in rehab Mary really started to believe that she could recover from her addiction she had heard so many stories from going outside to meetings of people who went through worse things than she did and have 15 and 20 years clean and more. It got to the place that she loved these speaker meetings that they went to every Friday, everyone had a different story on drugs and how they got started and how they found recovery through Alcoholic Anonymous or Narcotics Anonymous. The speakers all said that it was one day at a time that got them through with prayers, meetings, sponsors and other recovering addicts they told her it did not happen overnight but that it was a progressive process. Mary learned so much and after 1 ½ years in recovery she was allowed to come home for a weekend, she was thrilled and so was Charles. She told her husband that she did not want to know if he was unfaithful while she was away because she could understand that he was a man and she put herself in the situation that she was in. She told him she did not want to know either way if he did or if he did not she would love him no less and their marriage would be stronger than ever when she came home for good.

Six months went by fast and the next thing Mary knew they were preparing for graduation day which was a big event around the rehab. Everyone pitched in getting the place ready and the graduates talked a lot to the newcomers telling them about the challenges they would face and the rewards they would receive if they just followed the program and really wanted a new way of life then this was the best choice they had made so far in their life. Mary had met a lot of friends since coming into the facility, some that came with her, before her and after her and they all sat around and said how they would call each other and stay in touch because they were from different areas of the city and also different cities. Graduation was set for June 1994 and they were setting up for a big celebration, they would have the ceremony in the auditorium and the banquet in the dining hall, they had a DJ coming up and the food was being catered and each lady was allowed to invite 2 guests and Mary's two guests were Charles and Grandma Irene who was 99 and still getting around good, her mind was still sharp and she wanted to be there when her granddaughter graduated giving her all the support she could. The night of the celebration arrived and they were all dressed beautifully and just kept grinning and talking about how they could not believe this day was finally here. When their guests arrived they were shown into the auditorium and they made sure Grandma Irene was right up front because she was the oldest and would be able to see her granddaughter on stage. When they got to Mary's name and she came on stage to receive her certificate of completion Ms. Zilch said a few words about each girl, she said how Mary came into the program so broken and could not image staying there for 2 years with all these females. Ms. Zilch said that Mary was one of her best residence because she had never as long as she had been at that facility for over 20 years seen someone with so much potential go down so far and come back from what she has been through with such a positive attitude. She said that she truly believed that Mary would be one of the one's who made it and she congratulated Mary. Mary thanked her and began speaking by thanking God for saving her life and putting people like Ms. Zilch, her counselor Ms. Philips and some special girls that she could tell anything to and not be judged. She thanked her wonderful husband for his love and support and being a son to her grandma and a father to her children. She told everyone that her grandma was 99 years old and still living at home and cooking and doing things for herself and that she was going to make them proud. Mary said that she knew that God did not bring her this far and keep her family together for her to go back out in the streets using drugs and throwing God's gift back in his face. She also thanked her three beautiful children, Antoine, CJ and Net and made a promise to her family that she would always be there for them as long as she had breath and she thanked the founders of the Rehab for being there for ladies like her and smiled and left the stage. Mary got a standing ovation for her speech and she came down and joined her husband and Grandma Irene. After all the graduates received their certificates they went into the dining hall and had a wonderful feast of roast duck, wild rice, green beans, salad, hot rolls, jello mold and upside down pineapple cake. After the meal they danced and fellowshipped with each other met each other's family members and they all loved Grandma Irene because she was a pistol. They could not believe how young she looked and how alert she was and so very funny, she loved making them laugh with her stories of back in the day.

Part 4

When Mary and Charles came into the house the kids both ran to their mother and just hugged her and kissed her and Mary just cried and hugged her babies. She called Antoine on the phone and he told her he would be to visit her the next time he was home on leave, Antoine and been to college and was now in the Army station in Ft. Benning, Georgia and he liked the army life and told his mom that he wanted to make a career out of the army. Mary was so proud of her son and told him that his dad had done a wonderful job raising him and how she wished she could make up for the years that she was not in his life. Antoine told her she could make it up to him by being there for his brother and sister and that he always loved his mother and that his dad never talked bad about her even when she was out in the streets. Mary told her son she was grateful to his dad for being so sup portative and how God had blessed her with two men who were such good fathers in her life, she told him to pray for his family back home and that she would continue to pray to God to protect her children. They hung up with Mary telling her son that she would stay in close contact with him and would make sure that CJ and Net would write to him and tell him how they were doing in school and church. Mary help the children get ready for bed and tucked them in with a kiss goodnight, she had not been able to do that for years and when she left their room she just cried and cried just thinking about God giving her another chance to be a mother. She finally laid down with her husband exhausted from her long day but not too exhausted for her husband and after beautiful lovemaking with her husband she fell to sleep in his arms and had a dream about her and Charles at an NA meeting. The next day she woke up to the smell of bacon, Charles had made a big breakfast of bacon, egg omelets with apples in them, grits and cheese, toast and tea and juice. She told Charles that is what she wanted to do for the family but was so grateful that he just let her sleep in and did not let the kids wake her up, it was the smell of the bacon that did it. They sat around eating and catching up before Charles told them that they had to get ready for church and Mary was so glad to be going back to church with her family and her church family that never gave up on her. When they got to church everyone was so glad to see Mary and her family, no one was glad more than her mother-in-law, and her brother-in-laws and their family. Her father-in-law was also glad to see her but Mr. Brown was laid back and had always been but he had always been a family man and was glad to see Charles do so well with his family. After church the whole family went up to Charles's parents house to fellowship and have a family dinner. All the family pitched in and brought something to contribute to the big meal that Ms. Brown and her daughter-in-laws got in the kitchen and prepared for the children and husbands. They all sat around and talked and they called Cynthia who was so happy to hear from them and especially Mary. They exchanged numbers and said they would catch up, Cynthia told Mary that she had never stopped praying for her after she heard that she was out there like that. She said that her children were both doing great, James Jr. was making a career out of the navy and Carla worked for an insurance company and that she had a third son same age as CJ that she named Stuart after his dad. Neither one of her older children had married or had any children and Cynthia said she was grateful that they would not get tied down early like she did. After dessert they all said their good byes and headed for their homes, Mary was still tired from all the celebrations and a long day at church and time with the family, she took a long hot bath and read some of her literature while the family watched television downstairs. Mary thought of the last two years and still had to pinch herself to believe that she had such a wonderful and supportive family. She just began to talk to God and promised him that she would never pick up another drink or drug again, she had names and numbers to call if she ever thought about it and did not want to share with her husband what she was feeling. After a nice bubble bath, feeling so clean and refreshed she called her grandma and talked with her a long time and told her how she was feeling. Her grandma told her that she should call her Aunt Thelma whom she had been avoiding because of her drug use, so after hanging up with her grandma she called her Aunt Thelma and her aunt just cried for about 5 minutes before she could get herself together to talk with her niece, Aunt Thelma also told her that she had never stopped praying for her and was just so shocked that of all people Mary would get caught up in drugs. Mary told her aunt she was shocked herself but it happened so fast and she was really feeling sorry for herself after her marriage failed and she lost custody of her son she felt so worthless. Her aunt told her that the important thing now was that she was back on the right track and with God on her side everything would be fine. She told her aunt that they would try to drive down in a few months as soon as she got back on her feet she wanted to get a job and start helping her husband so it might not be until next year but that they would definitely be coming that way, her aunt thanked her for calling and told her niece she loved her dearly and they hung up asking God's blessings for both of them.

The next day after getting the kids off to school and Charles off to work Mary got out her little book with all the different NA meetings and picked out one that had a 10:00 meeting that was not far from the house, within walking distance. When she walked in someone greeted her and the door and said "welcome to Just For Today meeting" and they gave Mary their name and she told them her name. People were outside smoking cigarettes and talking and inside they were drinking coffee and sitting in chairs around the church basement. Mary picked up some literature and sat down, she did not drink coffee so she started reading some pamphlets about sponsorship and we do recovery. Five minutes before the meeting started someone read a statement about the meeting starting in five minutes and if you were holding any drugs or weapons to please take them outside because they wanted their meeting to be a safe place. In exactly 5 minutes the meeting started and they asked someone to read a pamphlet called who is an addict, and someone continued to read a pamphlet until they all were read. They then asked if anyone felt like using drugs today and wanted to talk about it, no one did and then they asked if this was your first NA meeting or your first meeting at this meeting to please stand and introduced yourself. Mary and a few more people stood up and introduced themselves and said that they were addicts and then they had minutes by the secretary and someone else told of what was happening for people in NA such as picnics, anniversaries and work shops. Then the person running the meeting introduced the speaker for the hour and the speaker said again what their name was and that they were an addict. The person speaking was a guy and he told how he got started on drugs and how he went to jail and robbed and stole to get the drug of his choice which was crack cocaine. He told how he stole of his sick mother who was dying from cancer and how when she did pass he could not make the funeral because he was somewhere with a pipe in his mouth sucking on it. He told how it was years before he could get his self together after going into rehab 6 times and coming right back out and use again. He told how he had been clean now for 10 years and he thanked God for giving him another chance and he had to make amends and forgive his self for what he had done to his mother. After the meeting a few people went up to him and told him how his story had given them hope, how they also did things that they were ashamed of and had a hard time forgiving themselves. At the end of the meeting they got in a circle and said the Serenity Prayer "God grant me the serenity to accept the things I cannot change, the courage to change the things I can and the wisdom to know the difference." Mary left and went home and felt so good about the meeting and she knew that she would be going to meetings with Charles because he was also involved in NA. She went home and got ground beef out of the freezer for dinner and began to wash some clothes and straighten up the house. She did the laundry and read the Bible and some literature and called her grandma and talked with her for a while and then it was time to put her spaghetti sauce on and wait for her family to come home. After everyone was home and they sat around and had dinner and talked about their day, Charles called his niece and asked her to come over and sit with the kids while he and Mary went to his regular Monday night NA meeting where he was a home group member and the secretary so he had to open up and set up the coffee and donuts before the meeting started. As people began to come in he introduced everyone to his wife and told them she was just out of rehab since the weekend and would need to get some phone numbers of females to give her some much needed support. Charles had a speaker coming in and after all the preliminaries he introduced the speaker as Florence from the home group of Diamond In the Ruff and Florence introduced herself again and said she was a grateful recovering addict. Florence began by saying how many was in her family and how her step father would come into the room with her and her sisters and rape them and that her mother knew about it but was scared of their stepfather. She would tell them "what goes on in this house stays in this house", Florence said she never said anything and neither of her sisters said anything. That's where the abuse started and she felt so bad about herself that she fell in with a rough crowd who would cut school and go and drink wine and later they graduated to marijuana. Then came the pills and then the cough syrup, Mary was caught up in her story especially the cough syrup, Florence went on to say that it was not long before the cough syrup was hard to get and then came the heroin and that she shot dope for 20 years, lost her son in a drive by shooting and then she had a daughter while she was getting high on heroin and it was just by the grace of God her daughter was born alright because he father was shooting dope right along with Florence. Then Florence's legs started to swell up real bad and she could hardly find a spot to shoot up because her veins were so messed up. She said she had gotten so sick that she could not get out of the bed and her daughter told her she was not going to sit there and watch her die and she called 911 and when the paramedics got there they saw she was not breathing and they did not want to touch her because she said she looked so bad sores on her from missing hits while getting high. Her daughter began to plead with the paramedics to please help her mother, don't just leave her there to die, but they refused to give her mouth to mouth. They wrapped themselves very well before lifting her up onto the stretcher and took her to the hospital and when they got her there the doctor took one look at her and searched for vital signs and they were able to bring her back with the fibula or and was able to get a heart beat and told her what a lucky girl she was that she got to the hospital when she did or they would not have been able to save her life. Florence said she knew that she was a miracle to be standing in front of them to tell her story because so many of her friends did not make it, many died in their addiction and she did not want that to be her story. She was able to go into a rehab facility and get herself together and be there for her daughter. She said her daughter finally had a mother that she could be proud of and not being teased by the kids that her mother was a dope fiend. Florence said when she woke she could hear the doctor explaining to a group of doctors standing around that she had sores on her body like that from her using heroin. Florence said the blood that they drew out of her they showed her it was so dark it was scary looking and they told her she should be glad she came when she did because she would not have lasted long in her shape. They did what they could for her and sent her to a Recovery center to get the help she needed to try and stay clean. Florence said she stayed in the rehab for 6 months and she had a lot of her old friends that had also been addicted and out in the streets with her and were now in NA and had been trying for years to try to get her to clean up her act and now they came to support her and took turns making sure that she got to meetings and moved out of her old neighborhood. She said she had been clean for 15 years and that her daughter went on to go to college and became a nurse and that her and the daughter's father both got clean and stayed clean and got married and was still helping others to do the same. At the end of her talk, Florence thanked God for giving her a chance at having a life again and told all the new comers that he could do the same for them they just had to pray and believe and continue to come to meetings and being around people who would be glad to help them stay clean and do the same thing for them and that she would be glad to give any of the females her phone number and they could call her. She said she was living proof of what God had done for her. Florence got a round of applause and Mary made sure she introduced herself to Florence and told her she was truly an inspiration to her and could she have her phone number. Florence gave Mary her phone number and after helping Charles clean up they went home talking about recovery and how blessed they felt that God blessed them to be a family again and both in recovery and they knew it was going to work because they were going to work it. They continued to go to meetings and Mary got Florence to be her sponsor and joined Charles's home group and they became the couple in recovery everyone admired. The months flew by and then it was Christmas and then 1995 New Year, they celebrated New Year at church and came home and had a big dinner of black eye peas cooked in smoked turkey, rice, sauerkraut, beef ribs, potato salad, corn bread and fried fish a traditional New Year's Dinner. They all wished each other Happy New Year, stood around holding hands and Charles prayed and thanked God for his family all being together and everyone went around in a circle and said what they were grateful for the year that just passed.

At the beginning of 1995 Mary started looking for a job and it was not long before she landed one with an Investment Firm paying very good money and Charles was still working for the city of New York and quickly moving up the ladder. It was not long before they wanted to get out of the city and move to the suburb so that the children would not be so surrounded by drugs and gangs. They moved to outskirts of New York close to where Mary use to live and by this time Anthony was no longer living in New York. He had moved to Cherry Hill, New Jersey with his family where his job took him and they remained friends, they did not hang out with each other's family but the remained friends because Antoine was in both his parents' lives. Mary and Charles both commuted to work daily and had to make sure things were running smooth for Grandma Irene and also attended meetings a few times a week for NA. Mary had a schedule of getting off work and going to her grandma's house before picking up Charles and they headed home, one night a week they would attend a meeting in the city and every Saturday at 1:00 pm they would attend their home group meeting. Mary began to sponsor a few girls and a lot of them had the same issues of housing, babysitting and jobs so Mary looked into opening up a Recovery House for them and staffing it with a few good NA girls to run it while she was working and taking care of her family. Mary was very smart business wise and looked into getting a grant to open up the Recovery House, she had to find a place and then have a meeting with the board before she could move forward. So Mary began shopping around and she wanted a place in the area where the girls had access to NA meetings and schools for their children, she wanted to make it so that if they had children they could bring them also. She also had to have a medical staff on duty to disperse pills to the girls and make sure they got regular check ups, because some of them did have problems related to drug use. As long as they did not have any real serious issues Mary planned on letting them stay at her facility and so she did all she had to do and got approved for a grant to open her Recovery House. On June 6, 1995 Grandma Irene turned 100 years old and they had a big celebration for her, they rented a beautiful hall, had a DJ, had the food which was delicious catered. Grandma Irene had all of her family, friends that she had made over the last 80 years that she had been in New York, all Charles's family and a few of Mary and Charles's recovering friends. Grandma Irene was in great shape, she still lived in the house with help by herself, she still played her numbers and would have a small drink or two every now and then. All of Mary's aunts and uncles and cousins came, her Aunt Thelma came from down south and Grandma Irene was just in her glory, she kept the party howling with her jokes and stories about down south and even stood up and did her little dance called picking the cherries and all the grand kids just howled. Antoine was able to make it in and that truly made her day because he was clearly her pick. Mary said the opening prayer for the party and she thanked God over and over for her Grandma and thanked her Grandma for all the support she gave her throughout the years. They danced and partied until 11 pm and took Grandma home after saying good bye to all their friends and family and also grandma's friends.

Part 5

The years flew by and Mary and Charles continued to grow and Charles opened up a Recovery House for men that he called Recovery House and it was just like Mary's which she called Free At Last except there were no children allowed to stay in his facility like the women facility. Mary and Charles went back to their community often and set up different programs to help the neighborhood, they had clothes and food distributions; they went to the homes of the elderly and did shopping, and cleaning, laundry and anything they needed. They got grants to fund these programs; they set up programs for the teenagers to clean up the neighborhoods, pick up trash and clean off graffiti and also had things for the teenagers to do to keep them off the streets. They opened up a center where they had basketball, games, taught the girls how to prepare meals, helping girls that had gotten pregnant out of wedlock to go back to school, or training programs and eventually get them into the work force and off of welfare. They had Net run some of the programs for the young girls and CJ worked with the young guys, the people all over North Brooklyn loved what they were doing for the neighborhood and every year they would reserve the National Park and have a big picnic. They had all kinds of donations from all over the city so it would be their big annual event, they gave away chicken, hot dogs, burgers, pop, salads, bake beans, cake and cookies and all the drinks and popcorn and potato chips. They had face painting, and small animals for the young children to play with, pet, ride the ponies and feed them, it was one of the city's biggest events that they had every year it got bigger each year. Antoine was living out of the country and he got married and had a son he name Antoine Jr, that same year in 1995 Net got pregnant and had a son she named Davon she married the guy and he was a great son-in-law named Lawrence so Mary and Charles were proud grandparents. In 1997 they had a son they name Rader and in 1998 they had a little girl they named Mya Lynn, Net said she always wanted 3 children just like her mother, two boys and a baby girl and she got what she wanted. Net's children were beautiful and they stole the heart of Mary and Charles. They called Charles Pop Pop and Mary they called GeGe. Net helped run the facility for the teenage mothers and their children, Mary let her have complete control of that facility because she was busy with Free At Last, her meetings which she did not neglect always sharing her story from the time she was 5 until the present. Anytime Mary told the story she would have other women who wanted to have her phone number or for her to be their sponsor and she tried to help them all, Charles would have to remind her that you are just one person with a lot on your plate and if you don't slow down we will have to have someone taking care of you. Mary knew Charles was right but she was so grateful for what God had done in her life she just wanted to give back what was so freely given to her. Early in 1999 they had to put Grandma Irene into a nursing home because she was getting to old even with help to stay by herself, it was harder for her to get around and a few times she left food on the stove cooking, you could not tell her at 104 she did not need to be around a stove trying to cook. So Mary and the kids would take turns going to the Nursing home to make sure she was taken good care of. Grandma Irene stayed in the nursing home for a year and two days before her 105th birthday she slept away peacefully at the nursing home, when Mary got the call she knew what it was she had visited her grandma the day before and all her grandma talked about was Heaven. She told Mary that she had a dream about Heaven and beautiful music was playing and there was just people all in white singing and praising God and she knew that not long she would be with those people singing and praising God. When Mary went to the nursing home to see her grandma she was still warm and had a beautiful smile on her face and Mary could feel her spirit in that room and she just cried and talked to her grandma and told her to tell daddy I love and miss him. Grandma Irene had a big funeral from knowing so many people since she came to New York 85 years ago with her husband and step children and Jacob came a few years later. Charles and Mary had a horse drawn carriage, the horses were white, there was over 50 cars with friends and family, Mary's pastor the Reverend Pinkett Jr from her church preached the funeral, he was the son of the original pastor of her church and the eulogy was beautiful. They let 12 white doves go at the gravesite and they rented a beautiful hall in Center City for the repast. Everyone sat around eating and fellowshipping and almost everyone had a Grandma Irene's story to tell from her good cooking to her famous dance "picking the cherries". Mary did not do a lot of crying she knew her grandma was in Heaven with the rest of her family and that her grandma had a long life and was not sick, was never in the hospital and did not take any pills. In 2001 Charles lost his mother, she had a stroke and did not live much longer and 6 months later he lost his oldest brother to cancer, he had lost his dad 10 years before that. All the rest of his family stayed in New York except a couple of James's children moved away his daughter to Chicago who with her family was doing very well his daughter got a job with a chemical company right out of college and still with them. His four sons are all doing well. Of course Cynthia never moved back to New York and her children stayed in Brooklyn and started families of their own and all did well. Mary never heard from her siblings after her dad died, but she did keep in touch with her Aunt Thelma and also visited her often.

In 2002 CJ met his future wife Nicole and on December 19, 2004 they welcomed their son Charles Matthew Brown III into the world and 3 years later on October 19, 2007 they had a beautiful baby girl they named Deniece Nichole Brown. They nicknamed the boy CJ just like his dad, the children grew up to be fine children and both were straight A students and was a blessing to us all. Antoine's son made a career out of the army just like his dad and Net's children all went to fine colleges and they were all smart. CJ is still running the facility for his dad because Charles semi-retired, the rehab center got to be real big and CJ hired help and continued to do the work his dad started. Likewise Net continued to run Free At Last for Mary and she also had to hire help because there was a real need in the city for addicted mothers raising their children as single parents. CJ and Net also ran the free food shelters and homeless rather they had drug problems or not, a lot of the people had mental problems so there was a great need for those programs also. Mary got grants for all of her programs and today they are still running smoothly with Charles and Mary in the background. Charles and Mary have travelled all over the world, they have been to Bahamas, Vegas, have taken the grandchildren to Disney World 6 or 7 times, also to Hilton Head, Myrtle Beach, Virginia Beach. In 2015 Charles and Mary retired in Hawaii.

Printed in the United States
By Bookmasters